cold, thin air

A Third Collection of Disturbing Narratives and Twisted Tales

C.K. Walker

ISBN: 1537236970
ISBN-13: 978-1537236971

DEDICATION

For Charlotte.
You know what you did.

TABLE OF CONTENTS

THE CHANDELIER

The year my mother and father were wed my father bought his wife a very beautiful Baccarat chandelier. It weighed around one ton and hung down two entire flights of stairs. Because it was so large my father searched the whole of Britain for an estate that could accommodate it. He chose a very old, palatial home in the Welsh countryside. The mansion was six stories in height and in the middle of the house was a tall, spiraled atrium with a glass ceiling. The stairs wrapped around the walls of the spire encircling the great chandelier at the top.

As far back as I can remember I would spend my days lying underneath the cascading crystals far above and watching the twinkling prisms catch the sunlight and cast vibrant, breathing rainbows across the walls. My mother would smile at me and giggle to my father behind her hands. I was a romantic, she whispered, a dreamer. Father would smile knowingly but never bother to glance my way. He only had eyes for my mother, at least until little George was born.

But I wasn't a dreamer, no, I fought sleep with every breath. I much preferred to spend my evenings dancing in the star fields that twinkled in the spire on clear nights. If moonlight shone into the great atrium it was transformed by the Baccarat into a million shimmering, twinkling tiny stars. The chandelier was always gently, slowly swaying without even a hint of a draft in the house, and it would make the crisp, vibrant celestials dance upon the wall to a song only I could hear. And I would dance in the star fields with them.

One day I awoke from an afternoon nap to the loud but sluggish groan of protesting metal. I arrived at the bannister just in time to see the Baccarat's metal supports snap in two. The chandelier fell half a story until it was brought to an abrupt and violent halt by its last remaining support - a thick, nylon rope. George was playing with a train set far below and I screamed to him. He looked up at me and I saw his sweet face for just a moment before he was obscured from my view. The nylon rope snapped and the chandelier went crashing down five stories to the bottom floor where my mother had thrown herself protectively over George.

My father would only shed his tears for them behind closed doors. I could not his pain, but I could hear my father's anguished sobs from behind the great oak doors of his study. A week after their deaths Father had the Baccarat repaired. A few days later, on a cold October night, the great chandelier was rehung. It had been my mother's and Father had loved her deeply. Perhaps he liked to look at the chandelier and think of her. But I preferred to imagine that he rehung it for me because he knew how much it meant to me.

But the chandelier was not the same. The gentle cadence it had loyally kept since my birth was now replaced by a stillness as absolute as death. The rainbows were dull, almost colorless. The dancing stars that had once glittered upon the walls at night were now absent, and the spiraled atrium remained as dark as the heart of obsidian.

I still spend my days and nights lying on the floor looking up at the chandelier and hoping its magic will return to me. Some days I can almost see the vibrant colors and speckled starlight. Most days I see nothing at all.

But nothing at all is better than the nightmare that creeps through the veil sometimes, cruel and uninvited. Sometimes I can feel the cold and the hunger and the pain in my chest. Sometimes the dark nights and dull days make sense. Sometimes I can see the Baccarat for what it really is. Because sometimes I remember that it wasn't the chandelier that my father hung at the top of the atrium that night - it was himself.

HOW DO YOU KILL A MONSTER?

"Ben? What are you doing in there?"

I briefly glanced up at the door where my wife stood on the other side.

"I'll just be another minute." There was no point in answering her question. She knew what I was doing, I'm sure. And she didn't like it. And she didn't understand. Because she wanted me to move on.

My eyes slid back down to my phone where they continued to watch the tiny screen for another four minutes. I had scoured the internet for months looking for the rest of the trial but all I could find was this aggressively edited six minute segment that had been televised by A Current Affair. I'd seen the video so many times I knew every detail of every second. But still I watched. Because I needed an answer.

The camera was currently focused on the jury. They were all leaning forward and concentrating on the testimony of a forensics expert. The camera then slid over to the witness stand where Dr. Felmore talked about the decomposition of Andrew's body and the state it had been in when a dog-walker had discovered it the previous May.

Felmore then walked over to the overhead projector, tapped a stack of slides on the table to straighten them, and then slid the top slide off of the stack and placed it on the projector. A graphic photo of Andrew's naked body suddenly assaulted the court and the entire room gasped. A Current Affair had blurred out the photo but I remembered what was on it. My poor little Andrew…it had been my job to protect him. They were right to be horrified. Listening to a monotone medical expert drone on about the graphic abuse of a five year old child was much different than seeing its effects first hand.

The doctor explained the slides without emotion, pointing out the countless abrasions, bruises, and open fractures. He spoke about the ultimate manner of death – strangulation - and showed the court how the handprints on Andrew's neck matched perfectly with the defendant's. Then he turned the projector off and began to speak to about his presumed time of death.

The camera pulled back at this point to show my family, quietly crying.

And then, finally, it panned over to the defendant's table. The boy sitting beside his lawyer looked downright bored. He flipped a pencil back and forth between his fingers and sighed loudly, every few seconds. This – this was the monster I wanted to kill. He seemed to feel that the camera was on him because he suddenly turned, looked straight into the camera, and smiled. It was a smug, intelligent smile. As if he wasn't afraid of the consequences. As if he believed it had all been worth it.

And in the end, I suppose he was right. The boy had

been sentenced incarceration until his majority and then another seven years after that. It was nothing. I knew better than anyone that it was less than nothing.

I looked over at the gun I had hidden under the sink. It now sat on the bathroom counter, begging me for justice. Was it too good of a death for a monster like this? It would be so easy. Too easy. Didn't justice require more? A manner of death similar to what my little brother had suffered all those years ago? Andrew had endured horrors no human should suffer. Days of it.

I looked back down at the tiny screen and watched the last few seconds of the video. The boy had suddenly sat up at rapt attention as some of the makeshift torture devices he'd built were brought out and placed on a table near the jury. My family was escorted from the courtroom and A Current Affair ended the segment there. But it didn't matter, because I remembered what had happened next.

The detective had held up each one of the devices for the jury to examine and I'd rocked back and forth in my seat next to my lawyer, giddy with pride at my gruesome creations.

Valerie knocked again. "Ben, are you coming to bed or not?"

But I was contemplating a much more important question, the only one that mattered. In truth, I knew how to kill a monster. I glanced over at the revolver on the counter. That part was easy. But the problem was more complex than that. Because how do you kill a monster when it's inside of you?

Walker

INTERSTATE 37

Emily had finally had enough. I'd thought she was in too deep, staring up from beneath the waves, slowly drowning in her sea of tragedy. But she'd finally had enough.

Their fight had almost killed her. She called me at 4am, begging for help as he broke down the door that separated them. I drove as fast as I could from the next state over. I found her sitting on her porch. He'd left for work, she said, but he'd be back soon for lunch. She was covered in angry purple bruises and dried blood. She refused the hospital. She only wanted escape.

She threw all of her belongings – a single backpack – into the trunk and begged me to let her drive the car. I was tired, so tired, so I said yes. I would have fallen asleep next to her, I'm sure, if it wasn't for the desperate way she drove, as if fleeing the devil himself.

I sighed in relief when we hit the interstate. It was a flat, lonely road, but it led home. She seemed to have calmed down. Her eyes darted less frequently to the rearview mirror. Her breathing slowed and her body relaxed back into the seat. Her bruises were starting to turn brown at the edges. My eyes fluttered shut in long seconds of micro-sleep.

I didn't feel the sudden jerk of the wheel or the violent swerve of the car. But I did feel the metal crush and snap as the car hit the concrete guard rail on the other side of the highway.

Surprisingly, I was mostly unhurt and could easily climb out of the passenger window - but Emily was pinned. She murmured that we must hide or he would find us. I looked down the empty stretch of sunburned highway and I knew no one was coming: not him and not help.

I gently released her body from the wreckage and pulled her out onto the road. She was able to walk although she was slow and carried a limp. We had few options; our phones were lost to the twisted metal of the misshapen car.

And so we walked.

We limped along for almost a mile in silence before she broke it. *He's coming.* She whispered. *He knows it was you I called. He's going to hurt us both and then he's going to drag me home.* I could only hug her and tell her not to worry. I prayed that help would come soon.

It was hours before we heard another car on the road. Sirens preceded the two ambulances by minutes but soon we saw them racing towards us under the hot, midday sun.

The first went screaming by as if chased by demons. The second ambulance passed a few minutes later: unhurried and subdued. I tried to flag it down but the driver never even looked at me. He didn't slow and so I ran after him.

I am yards away before I notice that Emily isn't

following. I turn to see her standing where I left her, staring at the retreating ambulances. Her face is a distressing shade of white in contrast to the plum-colored bruise around her left eye.

I turn to look back at the quiet ambulance as it disappears over the horizon.

"That was us." I hear her whisper but when I turn back around she is gone. My heart plummets down to my stomach because there is nowhere for her to go. I turn back to the ambulance but it is gone, too. The horizon has turned dark though it's barely noon. The air around me has chilled and the only sound in it is my labored breathing. I pull my sweatshirt tighter around my shoulders. *That was us,* she'd said.

And then I realize what she meant. And then I come to understand which ambulance was mine.

Walker

THE POCKET WATCH

When I was a kid there was nothing much to eat. I was the eldest of five and so it was my job to make sure that I always let my brothers and sisters eat before me. War was inching inward from the coast and as it marched toward our village, food began to grow scarce. Animals fled the area, or were slaughtered and consumed in panic.

My father was a wise and cautious man and so we waited to slaughter our six chickens until the fall, when grass and tree bark had become too hard to find or inedible. The other families knew we had chickens and father stayed up all night every night to watch over them. He had to kill at least one boy from a neighboring town who had gone mad with hunger and tried to burn down our small home with a lit branch.

When the chickens were naught but bones, and the bones had grown porous and brittle from Mother's many soups, my parents sent my two eldest siblings and I out to collect bugs and field mice for supper. We were hungry but not quite starving.

One morning we woke to the first frost. Father lamented that there was nothing left alive to eat and Mother cried. My parents began to discuss something in secret. It was days before I finally overheard their whispers. Father thought that perhaps he should go to the coast and sell Grandfather's pocket watch to one of the drunken but well-paid soldiers. I choked back my fear when I heard his words. Grandfather's pocket watch was the only thing we had of value and the only family heirloom my father had to pass down to me. But more than that, I was terrified. What if war came to our village while he was gone? I knew I was too young and weak to protect my mother and younger siblings. I couldn't let Father go.

On the day he was to leave I spent the morning begging my father to stay. He insisted it would be alright and promised to be back in one week. But I was so afraid. And so I did something I have regretted all these many years. While Father and Mother were outside preparing his satchel, I snuck into my parent's room and smashed the pocket watch under my foot. Then I placed it back in my father's half-rotted desk.

My mother found the pocket watch. She cried for days. Father did his best to comfort her as I watched them peel the leather from my father's boots and boil the hide for dinner. The next night Mother found a dead rat and boiled away the disease with the new fallen snow from outside. And the evening after that she filled our bellies with soup made from rat bones and more melted snow.

My little brother Albert kept everyone awake that night, crying out his starvation. He begged for all the things we'd eaten when we'd had a garden and animals – beef stew, white rolls, succulent corn and spiced lamb. He made all of our stomachs groan as he tortured us with his memories. I screamed at him to be quiet while Mother sobbed from her room.

Father got up to comfort Albert and stroked his hair for hours. Then he went back into his and mother's bedroom and shut the door behind him. Albert moaned until the thin light of dawn peeked through our threadbare curtains. I could hear Father in his room, tinkering with the watch. My hunger had by now outlived my fear of soldiers and I silently prayed that he could repair it.

Father worked on the pocket watch all through the day and into the night. Selia had found dead crickets in the walls of the abandoned bakery and as we ate them Father emerged from his bedroom with Mother right behind. The smile on his face was one I had almost forgotten since I had not seen it since the day my youngest sister was born. He told us that he had repaired Grandfather's watch and that he'd heard of a soldier encampment nearby. *Three days*, he promised us, *three days and I will return with carrots, and lamb, and rolls so big they'll fill your bellies for a year!*

We clapped our hands in delight and ran around our small, dirt yard with a delight and glee that seemed a foreign language now. Father said that we were all to help mother find beautiful things with which to dress the table. The next morning he gave us all a piece of rubber from the sole of Mother's shoes to chew on and sent us out on our mission after kissing us goodbye and promising to be back before we remembered that he had left at all.

We had such fun that day, gathering horseshoes and shards of broken glass. We threaded bits of twine through the horseshoes to hang above the table and tied the glass to the ends, hoping they would shimmer in the lamp light. We returned home as the sun set, happy with our days' work and eager to return to it tomorrow.

We weren't yet in sight of home when I first smelled it – onions, chicken broth, spiced lamb, even sweets! I ran as fast I could, dropping our table dressings carelessly along the way in my maddening pursuit of food. I burst through the door to find Mother at the stove, preparing our meal in silence. I threw my arms around her and asked if Father was home already.

Yes, my love. He had chance to meet a wealthy mercenary on the road who was only too happy to buy your grandfather's watch.

I hugged her even tighter and sat down at the table as my brothers and sisters came spilling through the doorway. They found their places quickly; hungry, expectant looks upon their faces. Mother brought over a steaming platter of spiced, boiled lamb. She nodded at us and we filled our hands with the rich meat, hardly bothering with our plates.

I asked Mother where Father was and she only shook her head and whispered, "He's tired now, darling."

After dinner we were sent to bed with full tummies, barely a word having been said by anyone since our dinner had been set to table. We ate our fill the next night and then the next and the next. And every night we asked Mother where Father was and every night she looked at her bedroom door while she whispered. "He's tired now, darlings, let him sleep."

But eventually our food stocks began to dwindle again, even though was had moved on. And as the delicious lamb was consumed so was Mother's health. Each day bled more out of her until we were left fighting over the last scraps of raw meat like animals while Mother lay weak and wilting nearby.

The first day I went again without food was the day that the satisfied, hazy ether began to lift and my memories of the past few days became…confusing.

I recalled that the spiced lamb I'd consumed with such ferocity had actually been sickly sweet and the accompaniments I had first smelled from afar had never been brought to table. There had been no broth, no bread, no sweets. Only the sweet, gray meat we had been filling our bellies with for days.

But in fact, I couldn't remember Mother eating anything at all in the days since Father had returned. Instead she had sat quietly next to us at the table, staring at the pile of shiny, silver meat we consumed with such fervor.

And Father, I couldn't recall hearing his voice since the morning he had left for the soldier encampment. His chair had sat empty, night after night, and as the peripherals of my memory formed shape, I couldn't be entirely sure he'd ever come home at all.

Frightened and starved, I didn't find sleep until the darkest hours of the night. The following morning when Mother emerged from her room I asked where Father had gone and told her I wanted the truth this time. Mother told me that Father had left to become a solider and then she sent us out back to peel bark off of the bushes in the forest. But my Father never returned.

Perhaps the reason I didn't realize what really happened back then was because it was too awful to consider…and I was so very hungry. Perhaps it's not something a child could ever accept. But as a grown man I began to wonder what really happened to Father.

Mother died a few days ago and in death she thrust upon me the truth of these events from my youth. She did it in such a way that I can be sure she hoped I would feel the pain of finally knowing what my fear had really cost.

From her stock of meager possessions Mother bequeathed to me a small, wooden box that contained nothing more than Grandfather's shiny pocket watch. It was still broken.

Perhaps she wanted me to remember it all: the only hope of our survival that I had smashed under my heel. My Father's last, loving hug before he sent us to collect dressings for the feast. That overly seasoned gray meat that had greeted us upon our return. And the rancid, stinging smell that had begun drifting out from under Mother's door after that day. My father had sacrificed more for his family than most could ever conceive.

I used to lament that I had nothing to remember him by. No photos, no diaries, no family heirloom to pass down to my own children.

But now I have his pocket watch, and it is a thing I cannot ever give to my children. Not because the glass is shattered. Not because the gears are cracked.

I cannot part with the watch because it is a curse that I must bear…for the contortion of gears and metal that hang from the chain still smells of that sweet, shiny, silver meat.

CHAR

I was the one who had set the fire. Everyone knew it, even her. Especially her.

When I heard the sirens I had run. I took a well-known shortcut through the woods to a carnival the next county over. But even miles away I couldn't escape the screaming. Not of the victims - but of their parents, whose anguished cries had followed me like footprints since I'd started the fire hours earlier.

She found me in the fun house, huddled in the corner of a room fitted wall to wall with distorted mirrors. She was my age, 15 or so, with wild, red hair and clothes that said she had a reputation. She smiled at me and offered her hand. I wordlessly refused it and she joined me on the floor.

"I know what you've done." She said simply.

I didn't reply. But I was comforted that I wasn't alone anymore.

"Everyone knows," she said, shrugging her shoulders.

The girl inched her skirt up to scratch her knee with chipped, black fingernails. "Even the police know. They're looking for you."

A loud, painful sob erupted from my chest. "Go away," I choked. But I didn't want her to.

"You killed a lot of people today, Jack. Most of them were only kids. They're going to arrest you and put you on trial. You'll have to face all those parents, you know, for what you've done."

"Just leave me alone." I whispered.

"They're going to execute you, Jackson."

"No they won't!" I screamed at her but she didn't seem to mind. "I'm 15. They wouldn't kill a 15 year old. Get away from me!"

She scooted closer and nodded in excitement. Her pale skin glistened with sweat.

"Oh, they will, I promise you. They'll try you as an adult and fry you black as bacon. But don't worry, I can help. I can fix all of this, Jackson. I can make it all go away." Her tongue darted out to eagerly lick the pink gloss from her lips.

I wanted to yell at her. I wanted to push her away from me. But I didn't want her to leave. I was afraid to be alone and she knew it.

"How- how could you help me?" I whispered.

She clapped her hands and giggled, then slapped her palm over her mouth as if she had just admitted a scandalous secret. Then she explained what she called "a simple transaction".

But it was far from simple. The girl promised that she would make the fire go away, as if it had never happened at all, and I would pay with the only currency I had – my soul.

With nothing to lose I agreed to her bargain. We shook on it. She offered me her body, some release if I wanted it but my stomach churned at the thought. The girl stood up then and again offered me her hand. I took it this time and she told me it was time to go.

I walked home in the dark, searching the night for sounds of sirens and tortured wails. I heard none. My town was quiet when I reached it. I turned down West Oak Street to find the elementary school still standing. I stumbled to my knees in the middle of the street and prayed my thanks to my guardian angel as I cried. All was as she'd promised.

Over time, I slowly forgot about the fire. It had happened in another life, one that no longer existed. But it never fully left my mind.

By the time I was 25 I had completed 640 hours of firefighter training and was hired by the local ladder. By 35 I had married the Chief's daughter and given her 2 beautiful children. But in the back of my mind I never forgot that someday the bill for my blissful happiness would come due. *But*, I argued with myself, *maybe not. I righted so many wrongs, saved so many people, paid my dues…*

It was a beautiful Wednesday afternoon in November that it all ended. There was nothing noteworthy or remarkable about it to suggest what it ultimately held for me. I had stopped at the mall on the way home from work to pick up a Christmas gift I had ordered for my wife, Emily. As I stood at the counter signing for my purchase I looked over to see a baby's stroller blocking the path out of the store. As the child shifted and the blanket fell from its misshapen head, I gasped.

I could only call it a monster. The child's skin was yellowed and leaking a white pus. It had only one eye, which swung from its eye socket like a pendulum when he turned his head. I stared at it in horror as the angry mother gave me a murderous look and hurried the child out of the store.

I took a moment to collect myself and then ran out after her, my desperate need to protect and atone driving my pursuit. I caught her in the food court and just as I reached out to grab her I felt a violent tug on my arm and I was spun around. I was confronted with a vision of horror and impossibility. The man who looked back at me was hardly a man at all. His body was a charred corpse from his feet to the top of his head where blackened skull showed through gray flakes of scorched flesh. He emitted a loud and dry hiss and his mouth worked in what I assumed were words as ash flaked off of his seared lips. Then he pushed me hard on my chest and went to stand by the woman who was almost in tears. Could she see the nightmare, too?

I backed away from the creature and his spawn and ran through the mall toward the parking lot. As the stores slipped by my peripheral vision I spotted four more charred corpses watching me, many holding the hands of tiny, yellowed, bulbous monsters.

I didn't stop running until I reached my car. I slammed the door and locked it, then sat crying in the front seat as the shadows around me grew longer and midday turned to afternoon.

I was having a breakdown. The horrors of the fire that was erased from time had finally caught up to me. I needed therapy. No, I needed more than therapy, I needed Emily.

As the hours ticked by and I failed to compose myself

to a useful degree I realized there was only one place I could go.

I threw my car in gear and sped across town to the only thing that could assuage my guilt. The school was still there - it had to be. I prayed it was. But as I came upon it all I found was a pile of rotting, burnt out debris. Lines of young children were filing out of the wreckage and making for the nearby school buses. They laughed and pushed each other around as if they didn't realize they were surrounded by the detritus of my sins.

And among them I saw lurking the misshapen, nebulous balls of pus and cartilage. The monsters were here, too.

The globose creatures ran to the cars of even more charred corpses, who hugged them and kissed them on what I assumed were their cheeks. Some of the burnt people recognized me. Some of them waved and pieces of charred flesh sloughed off of their arms. I wretched.

And I knew.

Somehow I had crossed over to the other timeline - the one that wasn't supposed to exist anymore. The one where I had killed so many children, burned them in their school in the middle of the day. And now the dead had grown up and had children of their own, children who were just a chaotic mass of cells and biologic matter because they were never meant to be.

This wasn't the deal! I screamed at her.

I knew she was nearby. And I knew she was listening. *They're supposed to be alive! They're supposed to be saved!*

It was the end and I knew it. She was giving me a taste of hell before she claimed me. I raced home to see my family one last time. I needed to hold them and tell them how much I loved them, a few moments to prepare me for an eternity in Hell. I knew my wife was okay. I knew she wasn't born until years after the fire. And I needed to see her beautiful face one more time.

I threw open the door and found her sitting in a chair by the window. She was reading her favorite novel again. Her skin was weeping and the thick, blood stained liquid fell upon the pages of the book. She shifted to look over at me and the bubbles of thin, unformed skin that covered her began to pop as they brushed against the arm chair. A putrid smell filled the room.

I backed away from her with a terrified cry. It wasn't possible. How could she be one of them? I was in agony. My beloved wife was too old to be the child of one of the dead students. It didn't make sense.

A car door slammed outside and I jerked towards the window to see a tall, blackened skeleton burned down to scorched bone. It was coming up the driveway with two ghoulish creatures following behind. And I knew it was my wife's father and my children.

I fell to my knees and let out an agonizing scream as the equation solved itself. So, he had been there, fighting the fire. He had burned to death that day and she was a creature that should never have existed. And so neither should our daughters.

I spared not another look for my family because I couldn't bare it. I ran to the bedroom that I shared with my wife and pulled a 9mm out of the closet, a gift from my father-in-law. I slid down the wall to sit on the floor and I leaned my head back against the burgundy wallpaper. I loaded the gun and suddenly she was in front of me, sitting cross-legged on the floor. She was wearing the same pink skirt from all those years ago and her hair still smelled like sweat and cotton candy. I knew she had come to collect what I owed. But that was okay. I was ready to leave this hell so that life on earth, life for my family, could go back to the beautiful thing it was before, albeit without me.

I'm ready to die. I told her. She giggled.

Release me from this pain. I begged.

The girl rolled her eyes and gestured to the gun in my hand. I nodded in understanding and as tears rolled down my face, I placed the 9mm in my mouth. I sent up a silent prayer that my wife and children would live happy lives after I was gone.

I squeezed the trigger and a hole blew out the back of my head. The girl laughed. I hastened to put the gun under my chin before the pain hit and crippled me. I pulled the trigger again and part of my face hit the wall next to me. I looked at her with the only eye I had left. She gave me a dull, disinterested smile. I unloaded the gun into my brain and she started to look downright bored.

And that was when I finally realized the truth: I wasn't going anywhere. Because I had never gone home that night, all those years ago. I had never even left the carnival.

She stood up without sparing me a look and walked out of the room, abandoning me to the hellish nightmare beyond the door. I could hear the guttural grunting and hissing of the monsters on the other side. And that's all they are now - monsters. I don't have a wife and children. I never did. Because now I've accepted it. Now I know.

She had come to help me, and she had fulfilled her end of the bargain. Because somewhere life had continued on without the event of the fire. I'd sold my soul to give it to them, to pay my debt to the parents of the dead.

But there was another debt to pay, that of my soul, and now I realized something that I didn't know then. Payment had been due at time of service.

THE THINGS WE SEE IN THE WOODS

I've been dead for decades. It took me years to realize it, though. And I didn't even really accept it until I'd finally found my way out of the woods and realized that I couldn't step out onto the road. It was almost like coming up against a glass wall. I could see the road, but I couldn't step onto it. Something was binding me to the miles and miles of trees and mountains.

I didn't meet Jeremy until the 1990's, I think. At least, that's what he told me. There is no real reference for time out here.

Jeremy was older than me by a few years and took far less time in accepting what had happened to him. He told me the story of his death the first night that I met him as we sat around a sad, pale fire that provided only light and no heat. There is no warmth for the dead.

Jeremy had gone hiking with his girlfriend one weekend, planning to propose to her on a mountain top (he told me he had hoped to salvage their heated but struggling relationship).

Unfortunately for Jeremy, his girlfriend had a nasty temper and during an argument on said mountain top, she had pushed him over the side of a cliff in a rage. Jeremy told me that he would never know if she meant to kill him or even if she knew how far down the ground had been behind him.

He had watched her wail on her knees as the rescue crews pulled his mangled body from the gorge. She was very upset that her beloved boyfriend had slipped and fallen to his death, and so soon after giving her such a beautiful diamond ring.

For as anticlimactic as Jeremy's short life had been, he was still upbeat most days and great company after I had been alone for so long. My favorite way to fall asleep at night was listening to Jeremy's stories from a world after 1983, the year that I had departed it.

We didn't need sleep, of course, but it was an effective way to pass the time. And there was so very much of that. Jeremy and I both still had the packs we had died wearing. Our gear never rusted and our clothes never seemed to show any signs of wear. It was as if *we* were frozen in time but it continued to move all around us.

We saw people, occasionally. Real, *living* people. I used to come into their camps and scream at them to pay attention to me, to hear me, but now that I wasn't alone all the time, I preferred to just observe them. Campers were my favorite thing to find.

They would talk about what was going on in the real world, outside of the forest, or they would tell ghost stories. My favorite ghost stories they told were the ones about us. Apparently, e*veryone* knew these woods were haunted, and sometimes, if you were lucky enough, you could even see a "spirit fire".

They said that if you followed the light and found the fire, you would see no one and nothing else around it. And this was how Jeremy and I realized that we could interact with the outside world in certain ways, the fires being the most effective. The other ways, such as breaking sticks and moving their stuff at night (which didn't always work), tended to scare people. We never met any other dead people in all the years we had spent in the woods, but we were both just happy to have each other.

It was early spring when we first noticed that something had entered the woods. We'd spent the winter walking along the entire perimeter of the forest, trying again to find a way out of it. Winter was the worst for us because there were hikers, no campers, and no animals. It was just us, all alone in the silence and the cold, with our dismal fires that never stayed lit and our sad, makeshift Christmas.

So we were both happy that spring was finally here. Jeremy had tolerated my desperate search for a way out of the woods for yet another year (he loved the forest), *and,* more importantly, campers would be arriving any day.

"We're almost back to Burn Rock," Jeremy said as he tossed more pine needles on our evening fire.

"I know," I sighed.

"Lindsey…this is the twelfth winter that we've done this. I really don't mind and I hate to bring this up again but maybe we should consider-"

"That there is no way out of the woods for us?"

He gave me a sympathetic yet pitying smile. I hated that smile. Jeremy had accepted his super unfair death and the afterlife without missing a step while I never could quite let it all go. I had been dead longer than he had so it really wasn't fair.

"This is such bullshit," I said. "What do you think it's like for dead people in the city? Do they get to go clubbing? Get drunk? Hang out with each other? Sleep in warm beds?"

"I can't imagine that they get to do any of those things." Jeremy laughed.

"And why not?"

"Linds, we light fires. We try to eat sometimes; hell, we've even tried drinking leftover whiskey we found at a campsite. Do you ever feel any less cold or hungry or sober than you were when you died?"

I pouted. "No."

"We're just...I don't know. We just have to make the best of it."

"Forever, Jeremy? Are we going to be out here forever?"

He shrugged. "Maybe. But it won't be like this for forever."

"Pfft."

"Think about, Linds, in all likeliness more people will die out here eventually which means more company. The city will expand, the government will sell this land to the highest bidding developer, and eventually you'll get your wish and we'll be back in the city."

"Maybe," I made swirling lines in the dirt with a stick that I had found. "In like a hundred years."

"We just have to entertain ourselves until then!"

"Doing what? We've explored almost every inch of

these woods! It's all the same, over and over and over."

"Except for Window Canyon."

"No." I said fiercely.

"Lindsey…"

"No."

"I just don't understand."

"Of course you don't, it's different for you."

Jeremy sighed, and then sat down and leaned against his pack. "I'm sorry, Linds. You know what might cheer you up? Let's go down to Red Leaf Road. That's where the campers usually come in this time of year and we could follow some if you want."

I smiled as I watched the fire lick at the top of my stick. "That could be fun. I like it when they leave marshmallows. I mean they taste like nothing but it's still fun to roast them."

"Atta-girl," Jeremy laughed as he tousled my hair. "And, hey, maybe someone will even bring their dog."

"Oh God, I hope so! I *love* dogs." Not only that, but dogs could *see* us. And the friendly ones even played with us.

"Do you remember when-"

Our fire went out. It was nothing that could be explained, even by dead people standards. One minute it was tall and healthy and in the next it was only smoke and embers.

"What the…how did…" I stammered.

Jeremy had shot to his feet. There was starlight but no moon that night so it was hard to see him when he moved.

"Jeremy!" I whispered for no other reason than the

moment seemed like a quiet one. "Where are you?"

"Hang on."

As my eyes adjusted to the dark, the shadows being cast by the starlight began to bleed into my vision. Jeremy was on the other side of our camp watching something in the distance. Whatever he was looking at must have been moving towards us because every few seconds he would take a step back. And then I saw it too - a shadow that moved between the trees. Slow and steady and confident, it moved like a floating ghost.

"Jeremy," I whispered to him, and pulled him back down to the ground to sit beside me. He wrapped his arms around me and placed his hand over my mouth.

The thing that had entered the woods brought with it an absolute silence as it passed. No wind, no rustling trees, no birds, no crickets, no crackling fire…

It passed on our right, walking through the edge of our camp. With my eyes well-adjusted now I noticed that all we could see was its shadow. It walked on long legs and its head skimmed the highest branches of the trees around us. It did not pause or slow down.

After it had gone, taking the dead silence with it, Jeremy removed his hand and stood up to relight the fire.

"What was that thing?" I asked him as he pulled out the matchbook that always seemed to have matches no matter how many times we tore them away.

"I don't know," he said, and as the fire sparked up and the light reached his face, I could see the fear and worry etched upon it.

"Have you ever seen anything like that before?"

"No. I've never seen anything like that. And humans

aren't that tall. That was…something else."

"Is it dangerous us, do you think?"

Jeremy sat down and propped one elbow on his knee as he chewed on a match between his lips. "No. No way," he said thoughtfully. "It didn't even look us, probably didn't notice us."

"What is it? What does it want?"

"No idea," he looked at me and shook his head. "But it didn't feel particularly…"

"It wasn't *not* evil." I said.

Jeremy laughed nervously and then looked back behind his shoulder where the shadow had gone. "There was definitely something negative and…wrong about it."

"Yeah but not…unnatural, you know? It seemed like it almost belonged out here."

"That's what worries me." Jeremy said.

Days later we had made it back to Red Leaf Road. We hadn't talked about the shadow since the night it had walked through our camp. Even though I was already dead, that thing had instilled in me a primitive, innate terror that had haunted what passed for thin dreams in the post-life state.

Jeremy was the first to see the hikers and I clapped my hands in joy when he yelled back to me that a group was unloading their car in the parking lot. When I caught up to him, Jeremy was leaning against a tree and smiling. We watched the group settle their packs and make last minute map corrections.

"Oh my God, oh my god! I love this time of year," I clapped again. "Did you catch their names? Or how long they're going to be out? Or where they're going?"

"Not yet," Jeremy laughed. "I've been watching the kids." He pointed out two little boys playing next to a red jeep. My excitement at seeing them soured almost immediately when I realized how old they were. Some kids, usually under five years old, can see and talk to us. These kids both must have been more like nine since they were carrying packs of their own.

"Any dogs?" I asked.

"Sorry," Jeremy said, and pulled me over to drape an arm around my shoulder.

The adults had a map spread out on the hood of a car and were arguing with each other and pointing to different points on the map.

"I hope they go to Christmas Lake!" I said excitedly. "I *love* Christmas Lake."

But as the campers argued two words kept striking out into the cold, morning air like lightning. *Window canyon.*

Hearing them say it was like taking a bullet. "Please no," I whispered. "Please no…" But by the time they had packed the map away I knew they had decided that was exactly where they were going.

Jeremy sighed. "We can follow them until-"

"No!" I said quickly. "No. I'm sorry. I'm so sorry, you can go with them if you want, Jeremy. I'll just wait here and-"

"Oh Lindsey, come on. We've been together for decades, when have I ever left you?"

We camped right there on the road that night and for four nights after that before another group showed up. But these were not campers - they were cops. Jeremy and I watched as they immediately road blocked the parking lot and began photographing the cars that the Window

Canyon group had arrived in.

"What's…what's going on?" I asked Jeremy.

"I don't know. I think something happened to that group of hikers." It wasn't long before we got our answer. From what we could peace together from the conversation we could overhear between the cops and search and rescue, the hiker's camp – tents, packs, food – had been found abandoned when SAR went looking for them. There was no sign of the group and SAR told police that they could keep their helicopters in the air for about a week to aid in the search.

"We can help," Jeremy said to me.

"How?"

"We can look for them. They might in our world now…some of them."

I swallowed. It was bittersweet, wasn't it? More company for us, but people had died just the same.

"Where do we go?" I asked.

"I saw the trail they took. If they went the route I would have taken, I can find their camp. If not, we just follow the rescue teams."

I nodded.

It took us only 2 days to find their campsite. They hadn't gotten far, nine miles maybe, most people with kids take it slower. The camp was occupied by two SAR officers. They stood against a tree talking and strategizing.

The SAR helicopters tore loudly across the sky above us. I hadn't seen them since Jeremy's death. We made a base camp that night – near the Window Canyon group's campsite. We lit no fires, only observed and waited. Surely the dead would come back to their camp. It would be the only thing they could think to do. But we saw no one.

We stayed at camp a few days, watching the search and waiting. But soon hope soured and the rescue mission became a recovery mission. We ventured out from camp then, hoping to find the dead. We looked long after SAR had left and the campsite had been cleared.

"Where are they?" I asked as we lit our first fire in days. We were still close to the missing hikers' camp, and we hoped they would see our fire – dead or alive.

"I don't get it," Jeremy said. "If SAR couldn't find them, that means we should have been able to but they're just…gone."

"Unless…" I sighed.

"Unless they're in Window Canyon." He finished for me.

"Maybe you could go in tomorrow and see."

"I won't leave you here alone." His tone left no room for argument but I made some anyway.

"Oh come on, what's gonna happen to me, Jeremy, I'm already dead." I laughed nervously. He looked up at me and smirked.

"Alright fine, I will go in at first light on a *day* hike. I'm not leaving you alone at night. Remember, Linds, that thing…it could still be out here."

I shivered even though I was always cold. "I won't argue with that."

Jeremy left at dawn and was back before twilight, as promised. There was something different about him when he returned. He was more *alive*, stupid as it sounds, more animated and excitable. I knew that Jeremy had always loved hiking and exploring. Taking Window Canyon away from him had been a dick move on my part. But there was just no way I could go into the canyon.

"There's no one down there." He said as he fell down beside the sad, little fire I had made. Jeremy was always better at making them.

"Well, what the hell? Where else could they have gone?"

He shook his head. "I don't know. But I have a bad feeling that that thing had something to do with this."

"Okay, so say it did, say it killed them. Why can't we find them?"

"I don't know." Jeremy replied.

"Those poor little boys." I sighed as Jeremy gathered more sticks for my pathetic fire. You'd think I would be better at building them seeing as how we'd built about 7,000 of them over the years.

"At least they're with their parents," Jeremy said, "wherever they are."

"My brother was about that age," I said idly. "The last time I saw him."

Jeremy's ears must have perked up because he dropped the bundle of wood he was holding. "Your brother?"

I never talked about my family. And Jeremy knew damn well why. "He was a cute kid," was all I said. "His name was Ben."

Jeremy smiled and picked up his sticks. He threw them over my shitty kindling pile and re-lit the sad, little pyre with the never-ending book of matches.

"You know you can tell me anything, Lindsey."

"I know."

"But you don't have to."

"I know."

To ease the moment Jeremy began talking about his brothers and their antics as kids, which apparently annoyed their mother to no end. Even thought I had heard the stories a million times before I found my laughter echoing through the empty woods all the same.

It happened too fast, in only a breath, just like the first time. But *this* time Jeremy seemed more prepared, almost expectative. The fire went out and in the same moment Jeremy was beside me, holding me still and pressing his lips to my ear. "Shhhh."

I could see it in the distance. The thing walked towards us through the trees, casting a tall shadow upon the trunks and branches. It seemed to move slower than the last time and the silence that accompanied it lasted longer. When it reached our camp it stopped at the edge. I squeezed Jeremy's arm as hard as I could without making a sound and he breathed into my ear "Don't move."

I hadn't planned on it. The shadow was dangerous, even to us. I could feel it.

It started moving again, walking around the embers of our fire. It stopped every few seconds as if tasting the air before moving on. When it had walked all the way around the fire it paused, and I knew in that second that it was looking at us. And then suddenly, it was walking again, out of our camp and back into the woods toward Window Canyon.

Jeremy kissed the top of my head and then let me go. I turned to him, panicked and wide eyed. "Jeremy!"

"I know, just breathe."

"It looked at us! Did you feel that?!"

"Yes."

"What was it doing?!"

"I think it was hunting."

"For *what?*" I threw my arms up and shot out of Jeremy's grasp to pace the camp while he rebuilt the fire for the third time.

"I could tell you my guess but you wouldn't like it, Linds."

"Humans? People?"

Jeremy nodded without looking at me.

"But we're not people, we're dead, we're just…" We always hesitated to use the 'G' word because it always sounded so…stupid.

"Ghosts?"

"Yes!"

"That's why it looked at us like we were leftover bones in a stewpot."

"Fuck!"

"My thoughts exactly."

I awoke the next morning to the whirling roar of a nearby helicopter. I hated the sound – it always meant bad things out here - but it was even less welcome now. Jeremy was already awake, standing next to the pile of ash that was our fire. He had his hands behind his back and he was looking up at the sky with concern.

"Did they resume the search?" I asked as I sat up.

"This is the 3rd one since dawn. I think they are looking for missing hikers."

"Our missing hikers?"

Jeremy offered me a hand to stand me up. "My guess is that there are *new* missing hikers."

The helicopters seemed to be circling an area known as Mill Motor Caverns. The caves were apparently very beautiful, though I'd never gone down there myself. I didn't like going underground anymore - it reminded me too much of being buried. Jeremy usually did the cave system about once a year on day hikes while we camped at the entrance.

"Oh shit."

Jeremy gave me a worried look.

"Should we go over there? See what we can learn? See if we can help?"

He nodded. "Although I don't know how much help we'll be."

"If they died-"

"Lindsey, that thing last night, it came from that direction. It was obviously over by the caverns at some point in the last few days."

"So you think...I mean you don't think..."

"I don't think we'll find them," he said grimly. "But we have to try, don't we?"

The new campsite looked exactly like the one outside of Window Canyon. It was abandoned, as if fled abruptly. There were tents, packs, even food that had clearly been cooking over a fire left behind.

"I didn't even know there were other people in the woods." I said.

"We were too busy looking for the Window Canyon

group." Jeremy shook his head. "Fuck, this can't go on."

This time SAR looked longer and harder than they had for the Window Canyon group. I could only imagine how badly they needed a win. But there was no sign of the hikers anywhere. Jeremy and I searched for them, shouting all day and making huge fires at night that only confused and frustrated the SAR teams. Eventually they gave up and left. We covered miles around their campsite in the days after but the woods were empty expect for us and the shadow.

At the end of a particularly long day we dropped our packs on the ground and fell into the dirt, disheartened and defeated. We laid in silence for many long minutes.

"Jeremy," I said finally, desperate to talk about anything other than our failure. "Why do we even wear these packs? We don't need food, or clothes, or pots and pans."

Jeremy was still breathing hard. "I wear it for you."

"For me?" I sat up and gave him a searching look. "Why?"

He propped himself up onto his elbows and wiped his forehead with the back of his sleeve. "Because you're not ready to let them go yet."

I raised an eyebrow at him and then laid back down. What did that even mean?

"I need a drink," I sighed.

"You and me both."

"A Zima."

"Lindsey, this isn't *hell*."

"Fine. A martini. I always wanted to try one of those

but I was never old enough. They looked so fancy."

Jeremy laughed.

"God, what are we going to do?" I said after a minute of comfortable silence.

"Nothing. There isn't much else we can do." He answered.

"People are going to keep coming in here and-"

"No they won't, thank God. I overheard Search and Rescue saying they were closing the forest lands until further notice."

"Oh." I put my hands behind my head and looked up at the stars. Being from the city myself, this was one view I never tired of. "Hey Jeremy."

"Yeah?"

"You know what I realized today?"

"What?"

"I've officially been dead longer than I was alive."

I had meant it as a 'hey listen to this funny fact' but as soon as the words were out of my mouth, cold tears were sliding down my stupid face. I tried to hide them but Jeremy knew me too well. He reached out and grabbed my hand and stroked it with his thumb.

"Hey, hey, it's okay. Hey, at least you weren't murdered."

I choked out a surprised laugh at that. Jeremy always knew how to make things better, usually at the expense of himself.

"Look, I'm sure that bitch did time," I said smiling, as I wiped the tears off my face.

"Oh yeah, I'm sure Miss Oh-Shit-I-Forgot-He-Had-

The-Ring-I-Better-Climb-Down-And-Get-It-Before-I-Go-Find-Help did lots of time."

I sat upright and looked over at him. "She did not!"

He nodded. "She sure did."

"You never told me that before!"

"I was saving it."

"Jeremy!"

"Look, I could hardly fault her. That ring could have paid for a very good defense attorney, if she ended up needing one."

"I wonder what happened to her." I mused, lying back down.

"She'd be in her 40's now. Probably married. Kids. Living the life."

"Does it ever bother you?"

Jeremy was silent for a few moments. "It used to."

"But not anymore?"

"No, because now I have you," he smiled at me. "She'll never have anything like you." I smiled back.

"Should we build a fire tonight?"

He shrugged. "Sure. If nothing else it's a good Phantom Warning system."

"Phantom, huh. I've been thinking of it as like a shadow, creature, man…thing."

"Your name is more eloquent," he laughed.

We decided to build a huge fire because we were both in good spirits and we hoped to draw any wandering lost souls that may be out there.

"I will be fucking pissed if that soulless, demon,

shadow, phantom-"

"-Creature man thing," Jeremy added.

"Creature man *thing* puts out this bitchin' fire tonight."

"Now say the whole thing."

"Soulless, black-"

"Nope."

"Soulless, demon, phantom-"

"Nope."

"Ugh! Soulless, demon, shadow, creature-"

"Nope!"

"Fuck you, then you do it!"

"Soulless-Demon-Shadow-Phantom-Creature-Man."

"You forgot 'Thing'."

"Dammit!"

Suddenly we heard voices. They were near our camp – and yelling.

"Hurry up!"

"Don't get too close!"

"Shut the fuck up, Jeff!"

They were on us before we even realized where they were coming from. Three people suddenly emerged from the woods – two guys and one girl. They all looked to be in their twenties and possibly, very drunk. Jeremy and I were already standing, backing away from them even though we knew they couldn't see us.

"Holy shit!" One of the guys said. "Look, no fucking gear, no equipment. Spirit fire!"

"Spirit fire!" The girl squealed.

"Ooooh no," I said. "No, no spirit fire."

"Do we put it out?" The other guys asked. "Or let it burn?"

I ran at him but Jeremy caught me around the waist before I got very far. "You put my fire out, kid, and I will throw you into the canyon!"

"Relax!" Jeremy said.

"No you don't put it *out*, you bush." The girl chided. "It's magical." She sank down next to it and stared, starry eyed and drunk.

"Please tell me these aren't missing hikers, Jeremy."

"I think not."

"We can fix that." I mumbled as one of the guys in the group started shoveling dirt onto our fire.

"Stupid ghosts!" He yelled. "You're gonna burn the whole fucking forest down!"

Jeremy narrowed his eyes at him. "Jackass."

"Mike, stop!" The girl yelled at him. "Why do you always have to be such a twat?"

"I'm sorry," he said. "I'm sorry, I'm really….really drunk."

"Speaking of," said the other guy, "we forgot the booze."

"Ahhhh camp is so far!" The other guy whined.

"It's not *that* far," the girl said.

"Jeremy, why are they out here? I thought you said the woods were closed."

"They are but look at them," he gestured. "They're idiots."

I rubbed my temples. Why headaches were a thing in the afterlife I would never understand. Ordinarily I would have been more than a little excited about finding people who wanted to interact with us but there was a wicked sharp knife in my stomach tearing my insides apart in fear for them.

"We have to get them to leave."

"We can try," Jeremy said. "But I don't know that this group is going to be scared by breaking sticks and misplaced packs."

"Can't we do more than that?"

He threw up his hands, exasperated. "I can't! Can you?"

"I can do plenty but I never know what they can see on their end and what is only on ours."

Jeremy sighed in frustration and ran his hands threw his hair. "We can…start a bunch of fires. Spell a word out maybe!"

"Ugh, Jeremy, that would take forever!"

"Fuck. I know."

"Let's leave the spirits to their campfire and head back to camp," the girl said cheerily. I've got rum and coke!"

"Well," said the drunk one. "You've got coke at least."

"Mike, you fucking suck, you drank my rum?!"

"Hey guys," said the other kid. "Since we sit around campfires and tell ghost stories, do you thing ghosts sit around campfires and tell human stories?"

"Yes." Jeremy and I both said at the same time.

The rest of their conversation was lost to the trees as they left back towards their camp.

"Huh, I figured they were camping down by the gorge or the caverns but the way they're heading…"

"They're going into Window Canyon." Jeremy finished.

I sighed and buried my head in my hands. "Of course they are."

"Lindsey…I don't…I don't know what to do. I don't know how to get them out of the forest without going to their campsite and even if I did go back into the canyon I don't know what to do once I get there."

"But that thing is coming for them. There's no one else in the woods, Jeremy. There's no one but us."

"Okay, just…just let me think."

"It's the fire, we have to use the fire." I said. "It's the best we've got."

"Ok, what- what should we do? Burn down the woods?"

"We live here!" I yelled at him.

"Okay! Okay, alright."

"Okay, we could…ah…oh! Oh, I know! We could empty out all their alcohol so they get bored and go home!"

"They're already drunk, Linds."

"But by the morning they'll be sober!"

"They may not have until morning," Jeremy said, narrowing his eyes at something out in the woods.

"Oh no. Please no," I shook my head. "Not now." But the fire had already gone out.

I ran to Jeremy where he stood, his eyes glued to the thing walking through the trees. It was slow and cumbersome, as if it was in no hurry. But it made confident, deliberate steps and its trajectory was pointed straight into Window Canyon.

"It's already hunting them," Jeremy whispered as it walked by, thirty meters from our camp.

"We have to warn those morons." I said.

"We will," Jeremy answered, sliding his eyes away from the phantom to look down at me. "Grab your pack, we're moving out. We can beat it to their camp if we're smart."

You can, I thought. *But I can't go into that canyon.*

"No packs," I said and Jeremy looked at me in surprise and let his bag fall off his shoulder to the ground.

"Are you sure?" He asked.

And I was surprised to find that I really was. "Yes, they'll just slow us down, now come on!"

We gave the phantom a wide berth and ran like hell for the canyon. Those kids were drunk and stupid and noisy and they would be easy pray for a creature like that.

The sky was fading into the dark purples and grays of dawn we neared the edge of Window Canyon. I didn't know what I was going to do where we got there, and before I knew it we arrived at the edge.

There was a defined and definite end of the path where the trail started down into the canyon. I was stopped on the other side looking at Jeremy who was already halfway down the trail. He skidded to a stop when he realized I was no longer behind him. He looked back at me but didn't say a word.

"I don't think I…"

His face held an expression like he was waiting for an answer to a very important question – and I guess he was. He was barely breathing, eyes wide in anticipation and emotion. I wondered if this was the look that his girlfriend had seen he had proposed to her, minutes before she pushed him to his death. Had she said yes? Or no? I suddenly realized that I had never asked him. Jeremy had offered me every detail of his life, even the most painful ones, for comfort and entertainment. And what had I given him back in all these long decades? My brother's name?

I knew I couldn't fail him in this one thing. I had to go with Jeremy. I had to go into the canyon or people were going die. Perhaps, worse than die.

Jeremy saw the emotions cross my face and when he realized I made a decision, he held out his hand to me. I took it and took my first step into the canyon since I had walked out of it over 30 years before.

"Stay with me. Don't split up. Don't look. If you see it, Lindsey…don't look."

I ran alongside him wondering where we were going. I wasn't familiar with this part of Window Canyon and I had no idea where the drunk hikers were camping. In the pale, muddy lightening of the morning sky I thought I could see smoke rising from the trees down below. It was at least two miles away, but I knew it could have been worse. Much worse. Window Canyon was sprawling.

We didn't speak as we ran and I tried to look only at the ground and think about anything other than where I was. But it was all I could think about.

I had spent the longest days of my life in this canyon, wandering aimlessly through the forest trying to find a way out of it; a way back to my family. It was just supposed to have been a day hike. A quick tour of the canyon on a beautiful, fall morning.

I had only left the trail to pee. Everyone stopped for

me and waited on the well-worn path as I tried to get far enough away that no one could see me or hear me. I hadn't gone far, really. But I never found that trail again. They didn't hear my cries and I didn't hear theirs. I walked for miles looking a trail – any trail at that point. I spent five cold nights sleeping under trees. I drank from a creek and gave myself diarrhea. I ate leaves. And then one night I laid down under an evergreen and I didn't get up again.

But I did finally find my way out of the canyon. I even found my way back to our campsite at Christmas Lake. But my family was gone. Everyone was gone. The snowfall had started.

And I did finally see a SAR team looking for me. But they wasn't a rescue operation. Only "recovery", I overheard them say. I followed them to the edge of the canyon every time. They never came out with a body. So I never went back in. The worst and last days of my life were spent in that canyon. And somewhere, in here, I still remain. I swallowed the sick in my throat. *Don't think about it. Stop thinking about it, you idiot.*

"I see them!" Jeremy yelled, and I looked up from the trail for the first time. "There they are!"

They were all sitting around their campfire. It was still mostly dark out, but thin rays of dawn were starting to peek through the trees as we rolled slowly toward the sun. "Get out!" I started screaming at them, waving my arms in the air. "Get out! Get out of here!"

"Lindsey!" Jeremy yelled at me. "They can't hear you."

"What do we do, what do we do?"

I paced around on the edge of their campsite, dry leaves and pine needles crunching under my converse. "They can't hear us, they can't see us. We make fires! We can make fires all over and they'll see them and freak out!"

"I don't have the matches."

"What?!"

"I'm sorry, I don't know, I may have dropped them or left them with the packs."

"Jeremy!"

"I know!"

Suddenly their fire went out. "What the fuck?" asked the kid who was not Mike.

The girl started laughing. "You build the shittiest fires ever Jeff. Maybe we should have stayed at the spirit fire."

"No, this is…that's impossible." Jeff said, truly perplexed.

"Who cares?" The kid named Mike asked. "It's basically morning anyway."

"Yeah but…"

"It's here," Jeremy said behind me. "It's coming."

I turned around and saw that the thing was indeed coming towards us through the trees. Its shadow was becoming hard to see and I wondered if it could be seen at all in the light of day. The canyon around us had gone eerily quiet. I turned to Jeremy to ask him what to do but he was already running toward the phantom and screaming at it.

"Hey! Hey you! What the fuck do you want? Get out of here! They're just kids!"

No older than us, I thought. I saw the creature lift an arm in the shadows and swing it at Jeremy throwing him 30 yards to his left. "Jeremy!" I screamed and ran after him as the phantom passed me and walked into the campsite.

I found him just as the kids started screaming. Most of their words I couldn't make out, but some were crystal clear.

"What is that?!"

"Mike!"

"What is that? What is that? Mike!"

"Mike!"

"Jeremy," I said when I reached him. "Jeremy, it's killing them." I was crying as I bent down to pick him up where he'd been thrown. I knew full well that you could still feel pain when you were dead. One of joys of the afterlife.

"Lindsey." Jeremy winced as he stumbled to his feet.

"It's killing them!" I cried. "I can hear it tearing them apart!"

"Shhh," Jeremy pulled me into him and covered my ears with his palms as if I was a child. I placed my hands over his and squeezed my eyes shut. With the absolute silence that accompanied the phantom everywhere it went, the screams and sounds of death were all that we could hear.

Suddenly Jeremy took his hands off of my face and yanked me around to run behind him. I noticed immediately that we were running behind the girl and the other kid, Jeff, who seemed to have survived. Mike was not with them.

As I ran I could hear the loud crashing and snapping of branches behind me as the great shadow chased us through the woods, hunting the two hikers that had escaped it.

We were running away from our campsite, away from our packs, deeper and deeper into the canyon. There was no way out; not for the kids, not for us, not for me in 1983 when I'd became lost back here. The only way out was back the way we came and there was only death behind us.

I suddenly skidded to halt and pull Jeremy off the trail.

"What are you doing?! We have to help them!"

"We can't! We can't! You already proved that!"

"We have to do something, Lindsey!"

"I know! I think we should do your idea."

"What idea?" He said as he bent down, hands on his knees, panting. "I should not have smoked so much when I was alive."

"Burn it down. Burn it all down." I gestured to the woods around us.

"The canyon?"

"The woods."

"Lindsey, I don't think that's possible. The canyon, maybe, it's really dry down here, surprisingly, but not the forest."

"If we burn the forest that thing would have no place to hide." I said.

"But we live here. You said so."

"We don't live anywhere, Jeremy," I sighed. "We're dead."

"What about the matches? I don't have them."

"I don't know!" I yelled back, and turned away from him to rub my face. But I did know. Because the matches were mine. I'd had them in death because they had been with me in life. Wrapped in a plastic bag, tugged inside the pocket of my jacket. One lit match in the right pile of leaves could set this entire canyon on fire.

"Come on," I said. "We're getting my matches."

"They're all the way back by the caverns!"

"Not those matches." I said darkly.

"Lindsey!" Jeremy stopped and whirled me around to face him. "You don't have to do this."

"Yes I do. Or they are going to die and then more people are going to die."

"Then let me do it."

"You don't know where to go."

Jeremy searched my face for a moment and then nodded. He took my hand again. "I'm with you all the way."

We weren't that far. And I had spent so much time wondering this part of the canyon in the days before my death that I knew the area better than any. We ran less than two miles before we came to a hill and I pointed down into the underbrush beneath the trees.

"It's there," I pointed. "Down there. Under all those leaves probably. Maybe even the dirt. Maybe even washed away," I choked on my last words.

"Let me." Jeremy said.

"No! No, you don't know. I have to show you, come on."

I skidded down the hill and ran into the first tree I could find. Jeremy came up behind me and I pointed to a large pine about ten feet away. There were no leaves there, only dirt and pine needles. But in between it all, buried underneath, I saw my bright green jacket, the very one I was currently wearing, turned brown and gray from age and the elements.

Jeremy took a step toward it and I stopped him. It had to be me. After all this time, it had to be me.

I approached the body and stopped to look up at the trees and sky that had been the last thing I ever saw before I closed my eyes that night. I knelt down and began to brush away the pine needles. The body was just a little bone now, and pieces of my jacket erupting up out of the dirt. I scraped away as much as I could but it was no use. I yanked on the bone as tears rolled down my face willing it to snap, willing to feel something other than horror and heartache. And then Jeremy was there, gently moving my hands away and digging into the dirt with his own. When it was free, he pulled out the jacket, which still held the old, yet undamaged, match book.

I hurried away from the body and Jeremy followed me back up the hill. He opened the matchbook and counted.

"15, but this book is not our never-ending match book."

"You know more about outdoor survival than me, you decide where to throw the matches."

"Lindsey. If this is going to work we need to split up. We need to set these fast, and in such a way that the blazed end up colliding and feeding each other."

"Just tell me what to do."

As we gained higher and higher ground, Jeremy pointed out seven areas in the canyon that he wanted me to set fire to. I looked down and for the first time since I go lost in the canyon in the days before my death I saw the beauty of it again. Of the river, Pony Rock, the lush, green, forest. It was a pity we were going to burn it all down. But there was something ugly in these woods, something evil. Jeremy kissed me on my head, squeezed my hand, and told me to meet him at Christmas Lake when I was done.

I ran as fast as I could, covering the miles in record speed, setting deliberate but hurried fires in all the places Jeremy had told me with my half of the ripped matchbook. The first three fires blazed huge and hungry but the forth fizzled out to nothing. I used another match and made sure to shove more dead pine needles on the fire this time. Then I grabbed the longest stick I could find, set it on fire, and ran for the fifth location setting alight every bush and tree along the way.

The last two fires caught hungrily and so easily that I didn't even need the matches. The sky turned dark gray with smoke as I ran for Christmas Lake. The fire seemed to follow me. No matter how far I got the flames were always close behind. I made it to the rim of the canyon and looked down into the fiery pit we had made. The gorge was filling with smoke and the flames were climbing up the sides of the mountains. "Nowhere left to hide, asshole." I took one last look down into the canyon and bolted toward Christmas Lake.

I had forgotten how easy it was to travel without a pack. I felt unburdened and free, as if I had been carrying my entire life in that stupid pack and now I was relieved of it all. It was a few miles to the lake but they passed quickly. I could see the fire still following me, although it moved slower and spread outward as far as I could see along the horizon. As I was watching the flames lick the sky behind me, I hit a rock with my shoe and went sprawling onto the forest floor. And in that one, still moment I finally heard it – the absolute silence. *Oh no.*

I rolled over and began searching the forest for movement. I could only assume that the sun was still rising in the sky since the black smoke had covered it as far as the eye could see and the only light was the distant flames that cast an orange glow on the trees around me. The dancing flames upon the bark made any other movement impossible to see.

And then my eyes found it, much closer than I had hoped. The tall outline of the phantom was standing right next to me. And then his arm was reaching out to me, and I was screaming. His long fingers caught me around the middle and they felt like shards of glass slicing me down to my spine. I screamed louder. I tried to struggle against him but his sharp fingers only seemed to dig in tighter. The shadow melted into matter and suddenly I was looking at the great, black, sinewy skin of the giant creature. He moved like he was made of wood and had no features upon his face other than a small, round mouth.

Lost, I was lost. I was about to be worse than dead. There would be no Jeremy where I was going. No trees, no lakes, no hated canyons, just oblivion…or worse. How had it found me? It had been running the other way, why would it turn to follow me? I was the bone in the empty stew pot. Why not follow the meat in the stew? Maybe because it was…fleeing. Maybe it was running away from the fire. Maybe it hated fire. Our fires always went out before it came close. So, maybe it more than hated fire – maybe it feared it.

Such a primal creature must have a primal foe. It only seemed to make sense in that moment, when all else fell away and the only other thing that existed was the crippling pain of the fingers. I found my pocket with a shaking hand and pulled out the matchbook. *Please work*. The creature squeezed even tighter, if that were possible, and his tiny mouth began to sink in on itself like a collapsing star until it was wide enough to fit my body inside.

I yanked both matches off the strip and, sending up a silent prayer to a god I knew didn't exist, I struck the matches against the strip and watched as they caught fire, then flung the orange glow into the creature's chest. It went up like a Christmas tree in March.

The phantom dropped me immediately and disappeared back into the transparent state it adopted when it was hunting. There were no screams from it, no floundering. It just stood there and burned up like all the trees behind it.

I pulled myself away from it, hand over hand, trying to get as far away as I could. I continued crawling until it was long behind me and the forest fire had caught up to the phantom and consumed whatever was left of it, which I doubted was very much because for a big, scary monster that creature was *highly* flammable.

Finally, as the pain subsided, I was able to start limping along toward Christmas Lake and that's how Jeremy found me, mere yards away from the spreading fire which had caught up to me.

"It's dead," I told him.

"What?! Are you sure?"

"I killed it myself." I pulled up my shirt to show him the long, angry tears in my flesh that wrapped around my entire body.

"Jesus, Lindsey!"

"I'll tell you about it just as soon as I sit for a while." I panted.

Since the shores of the crystal blue lake had come into view, I let Jeremy carry me the rest of the way.

"Looks like we succeeded in burning down the forest,"

I said as he set me down on the sand.

"Yeah," Jeremy said scratching his neck. "It's a lot drier than I thought it would be for the time of the year."

"You don't think it'll all burn down, do you?" I asked him.

"Oh no. I mean it spread a few more miles than I would have ever anticipated but there's no way, I mean look, you can't even see it anymore."

I looked back the way we had come and he was right. The sky was still black with smoke but the red-orange hue of the flames were nowhere to be seen along the horizon.

"Good. I would have felt terrible."

Jeremy gave me a terribly concerned look. "Tell me what happened."

By nightfall of the second night I was ready to move again. Jeremy thought we should stay at the lake for a few more days so I could recover but I needed information. How much of the forest had burned? Did firefighters get the blaze under control? Had anyone been hurt? Had anyone *died*?

We had to hike the entire night by moonlight but we finally made it to what remained of our fire. The canyon had been completed scorched and was even still burning in many places. The fires above the rim had been burned out or been doused by the time we reached the aptly named Burn Rock near the edge of the woods. It was the closest we could get to the road and fire crews to hear their conversations. We sat down on the ground on our side of the road and watched them until dawn crept in and morning gave way to noon.

We learned that the fires were all out or under control and that the two kids who can come screaming out of the woods "like bats outta hell" were both alive and being treated for trauma and exhaustion. We sat there for days - long after the fire were out, and even after the last response team had left our area.

In the days that we spent watching the firefighters from the side of the road, I had leaned on Jeremy's shoulder and told him everything about me – including the horrible, lonely, terrifying last days of my life. I talked about my eventual acceptance of the inevitability of my death and the entire day I had spent wandering around looking for the perfect place to lay down and die. It was the reason I had known the area where my body rested so well.

I told him about my family. How I believed they didn't look hard enough. How angry I was when SAR only showed up to recover my body so many days after I was already dead. I told him about the years before I had met him. When I wandered around, convinced that I was still alive, looking for a way out, and refusing to go back into the canyon - the only way I knew for sure had a road. Because if I went that way, I would find my body and then I would know. And I didn't want to know. But eventually, when no one could see or hear me, and it became obvious I could never leave the woods, I began to realize that I was dead and I was alone.

"And then I found you." I told Jeremy, giving him a cheeky smirk.

"How lucky for me." He rolled his eyes but his tone was amused. "Should we go try and find our packs?"

"No," I said, digging into the dirt with the toe of my shoe. "We don't really use them anyway."

"So where do you want to head now?"

I opened my mouth to tell him that I wanted to step out of this forest and walk back to civilization, of course. But it suddenly really wasn't true anymore. I didn't want to go back to the city and I didn't want to go home. Because there was nothing there for me. Everyone was old, everyone had moved on with their lives. And I didn't have a life, but…I felt a strange pull to move on anyway.

As I played in the dirt with my shoe I wondered about the gravel road that lay in front of me. It was still a road, that was to be sure, but what if it was more than that? What if it wasn't just a road for the living? What if it was my road, too? I could feel its pull on me, even now.

I stood up and Jeremy looked at me in surprise before climbing to his feet, too.

"Do you know where we're going?" He asked.

"No," I said. "But…I think that's okay."

Jeremy didn't say anything to that.

And then I took the first confident step I had taken since I had stepped off the trail away from my family decades before. And then I was in the road. But it wasn't the dirt and gravel it had been the moment before. It was brighter. And warmer.

I turned to look back at Jeremy with wide eyes but he was already standing beside me.

"You knew?"

"Yes."

"For how long?"

"A long time," he sighed happily and stretched in the warm light.

I let the brilliant, soothing warmth sink into me, all the way down to my bones and for the first time since I could remember, I wasn't cold or hungry.

"You could have left me at any time." I said, and it wasn't a question. It made sense, really. Jeremy didn't fight against his fate. Jeremy had understood that there was no longer any place for him in the world. He had accepted his death with the grace and dignity that was as ingrained in his soul as his DNA was in his body.

"No way. I needed a plus one for this party," he teased.

"Is this the 'other side'?" I asked him, laughing.

"No idea. But it's bright and warm, and I need a drink."

"You think there's booze there?" I raised an eyebrow and smiled.

"I can smell the mojitos from here."

"Hopefully no hangovers, though."

"Not where we're going, sweetheart."

I looked back at the forest that had been our home for so long. It looked so small now. The trees were swaying in the wind as if bidding farewell to their longest residents. I wondered if I would miss them.

"Are you ready?" Jeremy asked as he offered me an outstretched hand. And I was.

BURN

Hi Brian.

I know I should come see you more often but I never remember the visiting hours of this place. *Sigh*. It's no excuse, I know. I guess if I was honest I'd admit that this place depresses me. I'm sorry, that's a rude thing to say.

Well, anyway, my year was great. My son had his 2nd child, my 4th granddaughter. Her name is Emma. I've been pretty lonely since Lily left me so I got a dog in May. I named him BJ after you, Brian. He likes to go with me on walks around the lake. Let's see, what else…

My daughter got me cable and I spent a good, solid 5 days watching TV. You wouldn't believe what kind of shows they have now! I think a whole new genre is invented every year. It's a wonder I leave the house! But I do leave because, well…I have some news.

I met a woman over the summer. Her name is Holly. I asked her to marry me last month and wouldn't you know it, she said yes! I know what you're going to say: "that's too fast". But I think I love her and at my age there's no time to waste. Anyway, she is the reason I wanted to see you this year.

I knew it was only a matter of time before she asked about the burns. And shortly after I proposed to her, she did. I never told Lily the truth but I think I'm going to give honesty a try this go around. But before I tell her what really happened all those years ago I think I owe it to you to tell you the truth of the incident first. After all, you were there. I don't know how much you remember so I'll start at the beginning.

Do you remember how we met? My mother, a scandalous single woman in the 50's, was living with her mother in Chris River when I was born. That's where I met you, remember? You were trying to catch fish with a stick and one of your mother's earrings. I helped you dig for worms. We never caught anything but we quickly became the best of friends.

We were together every day, summer or school, Adam and Brian, always up to mischief. Our parents became friends. I loved living out in Chris River, all that farm land, all the wildlife. But then my mother met Richard and we moved far away to the city. I guess, looking back, it wasn't that far but as a kid I remember feeling like it was the other side of the planet.

I missed you a lot at first but I soon made friends and, I'm so sorry to admit this, Brian, but I started to forget about you a little bit. Things were getting better for me until my mother sat me down one day to tell me about your illness. I did pity you, Brian. When she offered to take me trick-or-treating in Chris River a few days later for Halloween I jumped at the chance. Brian and Adam, together again!

She tried to warn me about your condition but it didn't prepare me to see you like that. You were asleep when I walked in to your room and when I tried to wake you your mother stopped me. I remember being shocked when they told me you weren't allowed to trick-or-treat. I was so angry because no one told me I would be going alone. I had worked so hard on my vampire costume and now you wouldn't get to see it. And then my mother told me she wasn't going to drive me to the suburbs. I would be stuck going farm house to farm house collecting small handfuls of candy every other mile.

As I left I promised you that I would give you half my candy. I would trick-or-treat harder than I'd ever trick-or-treated before.

My mother gave me a pillowcase and told me to be back by 8PM. She then released me into the wild as the sun sunk into the horizon. Mom stayed in Nana's kitchen to chat and they both waved at me out the window as I set off down the dirt driveway.

First, I went to the MacArthur's, the Jackson's and the Whitten's. Those three houses took me over an hour and in the end I was frustrated to look in my bag and see that all I had to show for it was about a handful of tootsie rolls and dum-dums. Not enough to share, not at our age.

I then I went to the Nanfelt's and the McBride's. I started towards the Tilford's but I saw their porch light was off so I turned around before I'd gotten too far down their road.

I checked my Bugs Bunny watch and bit back tears when I saw I only had enough time for one more house. I looked down into my pillow case to take inventory again and said my first real swear word ever. Still not enough to share. I knew this next decision was crucial. After thinking about it for a few precious minutes I decided that my last house would be the Young's. I remembered that they were fairly well off and had a new baby so they were sure to be home and giving out candy.

I walked down Waddich Road for half a mile until I saw their giant, white house. I could see decorations in their yard and the porch lights blaring brightly to welcome hungry trick-or-treaters. I knew I'd made the right decision. I covered the rest of the half mile in record time, passing by only one other trick-or-treating family on the way, their bags heavy and their mouths smeared with chocolate. I hoped they'd found their fortunes at the Young house. I ran the rest of the way and took the porch steps two at a time.

I rang the doorbell and hopped from foot to foot, hardly containing my excitement. I heard footsteps inside and waited for the door to open. 10 seconds…15 seconds…20…but no one opened the door. I rung the bell again and this time saw someone peak out from the living room at me. I waved at them and smiled because this time I knew they had seen me. Another 30 seconds went by and my smile began to falter. I knocked on the door but heard and saw nothing more from within the house.

And then the porch lights went out.

I remember standing in shock for several long minutes. Had they given the rest of their candy to the family I'd passed on Waddich? Did they truly have nothing left for me? I was crestfallen. I didn't have time to go to another house. You are not supposed to have your porch lights on if you're not giving out candy, everybody knows that! I became irrational and angry and in my frenzied state I did something that has haunted me these last 60 years. This was the incident.

I picked up one of the Young's jack-o-lanterns and I flung it as far as I could into their corn field. With my weak little 8-year-old arms it didn't get very far and I saw it smash into the ground, a mess of orange pulp and seeds as the tea light rolled out onto the densely covered floor of dry corn husks and leaves.

It all went wrong so fast. I ran into the corn and tried to put the small fire out with my cape. I succeeded but burned my wrist badly. Then suddenly the dying embers ignited a nearby pile of dried leaves and began to creep up the corn stalks. I am ashamed to say I panicked and I ran. I remember grabbing my candy off the porch as I ran.

I fled from the Young house nursing my raw, red wrist and crying from the stinging pain of the burn. I looked back several times to see if there was smoke but it was difficult to tell in the quickly darkening night sky. And the further away I got the more I better I became at convincing myself I'd overreacted. The fire had been so small. Surely Mr. Young had already noticed and extinguished it. If it still burned I would hear firetrucks wouldn't I? The air would be warmer, wouldn't it? But the night was quiet and cold.

I did not share my candy with you that night. When I reached Nana's house I begged my mother to leave. I said I didn't feel good and that I thought I may have caught your illness. She felt my forehead and then kissed my grandmother goodbye as I pulled her out to her old, blue Datsun. I cried loudly and theatrically as we drove away, hoping to impress upon my mother our desperate need to get home. As she sped down State Road and onto the highway I chanced one look out of the rear window.

All along the horizon, just above the trees, the darkness of the night had taken on an almost imperceptible orange hue. I knew what it was and I was frightened. Just as I began to doubt myself I thought I saw a single flame lick up into sky and disappear as quickly as it had come leaving behind a sick, sinking feeling in my stomach. I fell back down into my seat and curled into a ball, moaning as hot tears stole down my face.

My mother was so worried she took me straight to the hospital. Richard met us there and he too became concerned at my panicked, hysterical state. I was shaking and crying uncontrollably, unable to utter ever one comprehendible word. The doctor was so concerned about my hysteria that he kept me overnight for observation. It was when I awoke in the morning that I first heard about the extent of the blaze. My mother and Richard were sleeping in the uncomfortable chairs by my cold, white bed and I could hear the nurses speaking right outside my door.

"It's so awful."

"We were ready to take on the rescued victims but there are so few."

"Yes, such a shame. What is the number at now?"

"18 dead. And there are still quite a few missing."

"How awful."

"Just dreadful, and the firemen are still fighting to get control of it, it's spread out of Chris River. It's been such a dry season."

"Do they know how it started?"

"I haven't heard. I do know they know *where* it started. Such a young family."

"Did all of them perish?"

"Yes, and so many more."

"Oh, stop Robin, I think I might cry."

I buried my head back under the covers and cried to myself. Soon my mother would wake up and she would hear what had happened in Chris River. Was Nana alright? Were you? Mother would know I had done it. She had seen the burns on my wrist, I know she had. I hadn't let the doctor see, but my mother had.

At some point I fell asleep again and I was shaken awake by Richard who bore a solemn expression. Mother was gone and he wouldn't tell me where, just shook his head sadly. He called a doctor to check on me and she looked me over, then discharged me. On the way home Richard told me that there had been a fire in Chris River and my illness, whatever it had been, may have saved I and my mother's life. He hugged me then.

Mother was sitting at the kitchen table when we arrived home. She felt my forehead, spoke quietly with Richard and then sat me down at the table and quietly told me that my grandmother had been taken by a quick spreading lethal wildfire that had consumed Chris River overnight. I asked about you. I think I loved you more than my grandmother.

I remember waiting for them to come take me away from my mother. I was so afraid of jail! But no one ever came. Adults whispered that a teenager in a witch costume was to blame for the fire. A witness had seen someone running from the Young's house at around 8 o'clock. But I wasn't a witch – I was a vampire without a cape.

As you can guess, they never found the witch. My mother stopped mentioning my grandmother around me and my wrist healed poorly. I never forgave myself though

I did try to forget about the Chris River fire and my part in it.

So you see, Brian, it was me that killed 22 people that night. It feels good to tell you after so many years. Thank you for being patient, 6 decades is a long time to wait for the truth. Mother has been dead for 15 years, as you know. She took my secret to her grave.

I've also brought this for you, the candy I promised you that night in 1963. These skittles will have to do as I have long since lost the candy from that Halloween. I'm sorry you can't eat them but I hope you will accept the gesture. I've also, of course, brought you this jack-o-lantern as I have done every year I've visited. I hope you don't find it in poor taste now, but it's our tradition and I couldn't bring myself to break it. I couldn't find a battery operated tealight this year so I'm lighting a real candle. I would be wary of all this grass but luckily it rained this morning. And it won't burn for long.

Sigh. Dammit, Brian, I wish things had been different. I wish you hadn't had the chicken pox that Halloween. I wish I hadn't gone to the Young house. I wish I got to see you every year on your birthday instead of the anniversary of your death.

I'm sorry, I have to go now. I'm going to a candlelit vigil with Holly in Chris River for the victims of the fire. Her father died fighting it, sadly. I go almost every year, after I visit you. I hope that you can forgive me someday. Now that I've told you the truth I probably won't visit anymore. I'm so sorry, Brian, I loved you like a brother. I hope to see you again, someday, if you'll have me. And wherever you are, Brian, Happy Halloween.

THE INTERROGATION

"How is it that you can't remember, David?"

"Because nothing happened."

"Someone died that day, though, didn't they?"

"I've already told you, there was no murder. No one died to my knowledge."

The one named Shaw braced his arms on the table in front of me and hung his head between his shoulders, mumbling to himself in obvious frustration.

"Alright," said the other one, called McNulty, from a darkened corner of the small room. "Why don't you tell us what you *do* remember?"

"Look, am I being arrested?"

"No, you're being questioned." From McNulty.

"I've been here for 7 hours now, I want to go home."

"You can't go home, Mr. Lancer."

"Then I want my lawyer. Have you called the number I gave you? Christian Bennett's office."

"We can't reach him."

"Give me my phone and I will call him."

"We don't have your phone."

I pounded my fist on the table and shot out of my chair. "Goddamn it, what game are you playing with me? I'm a citizen and I have rights!"

They continued to stare at me but said nothing. I crumbled back down into my chair and ran my hands through my hair. "I want to see my wife then."

The one named Shaw let out a slow sigh and then dragged his chair to the other corner of the room. He dropped down into it and kicked his legs up to rest his ankles on the doorknob and then pulled out a pack of smokes. "You know that's not an option, David."

"Why is it not an option?"

"Do you really not remember what happened?" McNulty asked.

"I've told you, I don't know what you're talking about. What I do remember is you guys showing up at my house and arresting me out of the blue."

"You aren't under arrest, David." Shaw said through the cigarette between his lips.

"I'm being detained against my will. If I'm not under arrest than I suppose this could be classified as kidnapping."

"Tell me about the party." McNulty said.

"I've told you everything I can remember about that party."

"You've been omitting important details, Mr. Lancer."

"I don't know what else you want to hear. Jen and I

showed up on time at the restaurant. We met our future daughter-in-law's parents. We had dinner, champagne, we celebrated Andrew's engagement for a few hours and then we went home."

"And then someone died."

"No one died! We ate, we drank, we paid the bill, and then Jen and I left!"

"And how much was the bill?" Asked Shaw.

"I don't remember. A little over $7,000, I think, there were a lot of people there."

"That's an awful lot of money for a dinner." McNulty said.

"It was my son's engagement party."

"And your daughter-in-law's parents didn't offer to chip in?"

"No. My wife and I are fairly well off and they are not. Some business they owned that went south. Her father made a big deal about letting us know, I think he hoped we would offer to settle the bill, which we did."

"And your son, Andrew, he didn't contribute either?"

"Why would he? Andrew and Maggie have only just graduated from college. They don't have a lot of money right now. I believe they are trying to get Maggie's student loans paid off."

"Let me ask you this: did your son ever ask you about your wealth? Has he taken an interest lately in your finances?" Shaw asked as he ground the cigarette out underneath his boot heel.

"No! And what does Andrew have to do with this?"

"Why don't you tell me what happened after you left

the restaurant." McNulty drawled.

"For the thousandth time, we went home and went to bed."

"Now tell us about the murder, David." Shaw said.

"I don't know how many other ways to tell you people this - THERE WAS NO MURDER. Jesus Christ, do I need a lawyer in here? Am I suspected of something?"

McNulty and Shaw exchanged a look.

"Mr. Lancer," McNulty stepped out from his dark corner but didn't unfold his arms. He seemed to regard me with distant amusement while Shaw stared intently through rings of smoke. If this was a game of Good Cop/Bad Cop, it was obvious who was who. "Did you see your son again that night?"

"No, I did not." I said through clenched teeth. "Why do you keep asking about Andrew? Did something…is Andrew…oh my God."

"Andrew is not the victim here, but you know that, don't you?"

I sighed in relief. "I don't know anything anymore."

"Did you see him again that night?" Shaw repeated.

"No," I said warily.

"Are you sure?"

"Yes, I'm sure I did not see Andrew again that night. Please, just, tell me what this is about. What happened to Andrew?"

"Your son is perfectly fine, Mr. Lancer. Perfectly alive, anyway." McNulty said.

"What the hell is that supposed to mean?"

"Are you sure you don't remember seeing your son

again that night?"

"I did not see Andrew again that night!" But then, right at that moment, my words became untrue. Andrew's face appeared in my mind's eye, and from a scene I couldn't remember taking place. He had emerged from the dark, pale and frightened, holding something that wasn't quite in the frame.

"Do you remember the murder, David?"

And then sound bled into the scene, too. A ragged breath from him, like tearing paper. A surprised utterance of his name from me. A burdened grunt, an unexpected crack in the darkness, and footsteps running up the stairs. And then I remembered it all suddenly falling away from me.

"Do you remember who died that night?" McNulty asked leaning against the wall next to the window. He was looking out of it into the darkness, into a world that I had failed to notice in my long hours in this room, or, perhaps, had tried not to. A world made only of sharp, gray angles and raw, white corners, a world without colors or curves.

"Yes, I think I do remember." I said, staring out the same window, waiting for a sun that should have risen hours ago. "It was me."

Walker

THE TALL MAN

We had all liked Mr. Winscot. He didn't mind when we used the sledding hill on his property and he always gave out the best Halloween candy in the neighborhood. So when we heard he'd been taken by the Tall Man everyone was really bummed out.

You wouldn't have heard of Tall Man, of course, so let me explain. Tall Man has been a legend in my town for *decades*. Those who claim to have seen him say that he is over 9 feet tall, slight, and pale, with an exceedingly polite smile. My dad told me that Tall Man is a collector; he likes things. Dad says his favorite things to take are sad people, empty buildings, and dreams. I have to admit he's stolen away my dreams more than a few times.

When Mr. Winscot didn't show up to church on Sunday, nobody thought it was weird. Then when Monday rolled around and he wasn't at work with my dad, people started to whisper. My parents thought it was odd but not particularly concerning. But then the rumors started that Tall Man had gotten Mr. Winscot. A kid in my class even said that he had seen Tall Man in Mr. Winscot's house through a window. I told my parents what Jake had seen but they only laughed.

Tyler and I biked by Mr. Winscot's place every day after school to get to our friend Rory's house. We never stopped in front of Mr. Winscot's to try and see Tall Man through the windows like Jake had. We never even slowed down.

But one day we played too late at Rory's. Since we didn't want to bike home in the dark we called our parents and asked to sleep over. Tyler was allowed to. But I wasn't.

I tried really hard not to look as I biked by Mr. Winscot's cul-de-sac. I almost made it, but my curiosity forced a backwards glance at the house. The lights were all on and my eyes were drawn to the face in the window immediately. I saw the Tall Man looking back at me. I choked in a panicked breath and my foot missed the pedal as I tried to speed away on my bike. I stumbled for only a second - my eyes never leaving the face in the window – before I pedaled home as fast as I could.

The next morning at school I told Rory and Tyler about Tall Man. They didn't believe me, of course, they hadn't believed Jake either. I knew I had to show them or they would think I was a liar. We waited until dark and then biked to Mr. Winscot's cul-de-sac. Tall Man was there – as I told them he'd be - watching us from the window above the front door. It was such a tall front door that I thought Tall Man must be 10 feet high to see out of the window above it. He was almost smiling but his expression betrayed a certain displeasure. Tyler fell off of his bike.

"Holy shit! Run!" He said. And we did.

As soon as we cleared the cul-de-sac we all began

talking over each other in a flustered panic.

"I can't believe we saw Tall Man!"

"Did you see the look on his face?!"

"We have to tell the cops!"

We went back the next morning with more friends but Tall Man was gone. We went back the following day, too, but again could see no one behind the window. We began to wonder if Tall Man only came out at night. A few nights later, as we sat in Rory's basement waiting for a pizza to arrive, we decided to sneak out and see if our theory was true.

We quietly rolled our bikes down the driveway and into the street. We took off for Mr. Winscot's house, torn between hoping Tall Man was there, and praying that he wasn't.

We saw him as soon as we biked into the cul-de-sac. He was still standing there after all, and this time Tall Man was outright frowning.

"He's mad," Rory said. "He wants us to stay away."

"I don't get why he only comes out at night." Tyler said while he snapped a picture.

"Don't!" I hissed. "Stop taking pictures, you'll make him madder."

"Maybe he watches us in the daytime, too." Rory shrugged. "Maybe we can only see him at night because that's when the porch lights come on and shine right in the window."

It was a chilling thought. We decided to test Rory's theory the following Saturday, emboldened by the assumption that Tall Man could only watch us but never come out.

As soon as the sun came up that morning we biked to Mr. Winscot's. We had to get close, almost all the way to the beginning of his driveway, but Tyler swore he saw Tall Man still standing in the window.

I made hand binoculars and squinted at the window for a few more minutes before Tyler suddenly said "Let's go," hopped back on his bike, and pedaled off. We caught up to him a few blocks later.

"What the hell was that!" I yelled.

"It was…Tall Man was there, but he looked different this time."

"Like how?" Rory asked.

"I don't know, he looked angry or just…wrong somehow."

It was days before we could convince Tyler to go back to Tall Man's house, and even then he insisted on taking his teenage brother Matt with us. Matt wasn't impressed with our stories at all. He didn't believe us, but he came anyway for Tyler's sake.

As soon as we got close enough to see Tall Man in the window above the door Matt got off his bike. He stared and squinted, and stared some more. He got closer, closer than we had ever dared to go at night. We followed nervously behind him.

Matt walked up the driveway and then down the stone path to the front porch. We dared not follow that far. Then Matt went up the porch stairs, right up to the door.

"Holy…fuck." He said. Then a few more four letter words, and suddenly Matt was running down the front porch, down the path, down the driveway and out into the street where we waited.

"What is it?" Tyler asked him.

"There is no Tall Man." He said, out of breath. "Call the cops. Now."

And he was right, it wasn't Tall Man after all. We stayed long enough to watch the police break down the door and cut the rotting corpse of Mr. Winscot from the ceiling where he had hung himself from a lamp fixture in his foyer. The body had decayed as if it were melting in the days we had watched it from the road. Mr. Winscot had written no note and made no goodbyes, leaving behind only the sad story of a divorced, middle-aged man suffering from a sad, well-hidden depression.

It was weeks before the town lost interest in the tragic suicide and months before kids stopped asking us to describe the body in all of its gory detail. Eventually even Tyler and Rory and stopped talking about it. Everyone had moved on. Everyone except me.

See, there was one detail that always bothered me, one thing I never told Rory or Tyler. It was about the first time I'd seen Tall Man, the time I'd been alone. The thing was, I'd *seen* Mr. Winscot that night: he'd been sitting alone in his kitchen eating dinner. But I'd seen something else, too. In the upstairs bedroom window there had been an impossibly tall, impossibly pale man staring back at me through the glass. And he'd been politely smiling.

STEVEN

Bradley stared at the TV in disbelief. It was always on since Marie didn't work and spent nearly all of her time watching Headline News. Nancy Grace was her favorite.

He'd heard the name of his small town roll idly off of Grace's shrill, southern tongue. His blood had turned to ice. *God, no. Please no. Not another one. Not again.*

"Another girl missing? After all this time?" Bradley whispered as he struggled to draw air into his lungs.

"This little ten year old girl was stolen out of her home on the evening of the 12th as she slept in her pink, princess bed. Beautiful, slight, she stands about 4 feet, 9 inches. Can we get a picture up, Jonathan?"

Bradley's heart dropped as the image of pure innocence filled the screen. A little girl leading a horse around a paddock. Blonde haired. Blue eyed. Just like he'd liked them.

"Is it Steven? Has he done this again? Marie, please tell me it's not Steven. Tell me it's not him! How did he get out of prison? Please, God, no, not again."

Bradley's wife sat weeping on the couch. She didn't need to answer him. He knew she believed it was his son.

Bradley waited a few days to call the prison. He hoped the girl would turn up, safe and sound, but the search for her had only widened. By the 10th day he knew he needed to tell someone to look at Steven as a suspect.

When he called he asked to speak with the District Attorney who had prosecuted his son all those years ago.

"I'm sorry Mr. Schow, I would have thought you'd been contacted. Steven was given a new trial six years ago due to ineffective council. He was acquitted of both murders."

Bradley hung up and finally accepted the truth. He knew his son had taken the missing girl and he knew if he didn't say something soon, other girls would soon follow. Steven was out of prison now. The system had failed these poor, murdered girls.

That night Bradley broke the news to his wife. They enjoyed one last quiet night together before their lives descended into Hell. Bradley dreaded the circus that he was to endure once again. His first wife had left him during Steven's trial out of shame. He wondered if Marie would do the same.

Bradley called the city police department the next morning. They arrived at his house later that afternoon. Bradley didn't like it when they separated him from his wife and took him to the station for questioning. He spent hours with them, repeating himself over and over. *Look at Steven, look at my son.* But they only told him that evidence suggested his son had been framed.

Around eight o'clock Bradley broke down and

screamed for Marie into the dark hours of the night. She was 2 floors below him in the morgue where a medical examiner tried his hardest not to cry as he autopsied the decaying body of the ten year old girl.

Walker

LAKE KAGACHANTE

I held the phone against my shoulder and I rubbed the corner of my eye socket. "Mom…"

"Casey, please, it's already been arranged. Your father will pick you up from the bus station."

"Mom."

"And the Anderson's brought their dogs! You *love* those pups."

"Ma."

"Plus it's a holiday weekend and Casey, we just…your dad rented the boat *for you*. Please come. Bring Ben!"

I sighed into the phone. I loved my parents but the last thing I wanted to do at that moment was go on a weekend holiday - *especially* with Ben. "Any other weekend, Mom. If it was any other weekend I would go."

"What's wrong, sweetie? Don't you want to see us? Dad bought fireworks, too."

"Yeah, I just…it's not a good time."

"I thought finals were over?"

"They are."

"Well, remember I tried. Don't be jealous of all the fun pictures you see on my Face Page."

"Face*book*, Ma."

"Yes, Spacebook. Love you sweetie – let us know as soon as you change your mind. And bring Ben with you!"

"Love you too, Mom. Bye."

I hung up the phone and turned around to find Nicole shaking her head at me from where she sat at her desk. "Task, tsk, Casey Grace."

"What?" I said. "You know I love my parents. I just don't want to go up to the lake right now."

"Why not? You love Lake Calhoun and you haven't seen your parents since Christmas. I could literally *feel* your mom's disappointment through the phone."

I shrugged. "She'll get over it. I promised to go up another time."

"I heard. How much of this has to do with Ben?"

"Are you kidding, it has everything to do with Ben. My parents love Ben." I flopped down into an easy chair and propped my feet up on the window sill, looking down at the campus seven stories below.

"Well, you have to tell them sometime." Nicole said.

"I'll tell them eventually. But not today. Today is for drinking."

Nicole shut her laptop. "Now you're talking."

*

The call came late on Sunday afternoon. I was lying in

bed, drifting in between Netflix and sleep. A half empty water bottle lay next to me but I couldn't find the energy to lift my head and drink it. Nicole was across there room snoring like a derailed train.

The piercing ring of my phone lit up the silence like a flash bomb. I pushed my fingers in on my temples and then threw the TV remote at the android which lay on the floor several feet away.

"Shut up!"

The phone cut off mid-song as if obeying my command but not a minute later the voice of MC Chris sliced through the silence again to torment me. I rolled off of my bed with an *oaf* and slowly dragged myself across the room. When I was within arm's reach of the phone I collapsed in front of it.

I flipped it over and hit *answer* without bothering to check the caller ID. Then I laid my head down on the floor and closed my eyes.

"Hello?" I moaned.

"Casey?"

"Yeah, isme. It's me. Yeah." Silence on the other end of the line. "Hello?"

"You sound terrible. Did I wake you?"

"Sort of."

"Casey, it's 4 o'clock in the afternoon."

"Thanks for the update, Big Ben." I murmured.

"Casey Grace Milliard!"

Shit. "Aunt Evie?" I opened my eyes and sat up on my elbows.

"Yes, of course it's me! Casey," she sighed.

"I...your...I really don't know what to say."

I rubbed my face and tried to concentrate. "Okay."

"Sweetheart, you know your parents were at the lake this weekend. You remember that, right?"

"Yep."

"Well, honey...there was an accident."

"Accident?" What did that mean? Why was she calling me?

"Casey, your parents were in an accident at Lake Calhoun with another boat. A kid, some drunk, stupid kid, he hit your parents' boat. It's just awful."

"My parents don't have a boat." I said thickly and laid my head back down on the floor. "That's a crazy story, Aunt Evie."

"They rented the boat, Casey! Are you drunk?"

"No. Maybe."

"Sweetheart, your parents, they...they didn't survive the accident."

"What?" *No, that wasn't right.*

"I'm so sorry. Casey, you need to come home."

*

The funeral took place on a Wednesday and cost more than I could have ever afforded on my own. Aunt Evie covered most of the expenses with her own money. In fact, my dad's sister had stepped in and organized the entire thing - God knew I hadn't been any help.

I was completely numb the entire day. I tried to concentrate on what people were saying to me but it was exhausting so I developed a few stock replies to their condolences.

Yes. Thank you. It's going okay. I love you, too. Thank you for coming. My mom always loved you.

At the end of the short service everyone stood up to follow the pallbearers out of the church. I stared into my lap, as I had for most of the day, and played with the rings on my left hand while trying to conjure the energy to follow them out to the burial plots.

I felt someone sit down next to me and take my hand. My Aunt Evie was a beautiful woman of 53 with platinum blonde hair and bright, green eyes. But today she looked tired, sad, and even a little haggard.

"Casey… How are you doing?"

I laid my head against on her delicate shoulder. "You know I was thinking today that you're the only family I have left."

She patted my hand. "I will work my hardest to make sure that I'm enough. You're the only family I have left, too."

It was true. Aunt Evie had been married once but her husband left her when she couldn't produce children for him. Evie's infertility had always been her greatest heartache.

"Sweetheart…I don't really know if there's a good time to bring this up but did you know that I'm the executor of your parents' estate?"

"I guess that makes sense."

Evie said nothing.

"Well, I just want the house. The house I grew up in. That's all I care about. The rest…" I waved my hand dismissively.

Evie sat me up. "Honey, you know, your parents lost

that house years ago. From what I understand they worked out a deal to rent but…sweetie, the house isn't theirs to give."

It was like taking a bullet while I was already bleeding on the ground.

"Why don't you let me speak to the homeowner and maybe he will sell the house back to you. Your father's life insurance should pay out quite a bit."

"Okay, yes, fine, do whatever, I just want our house. I was- I was going to take the summer off and stay there. I feel closer to them there." A felt a single tear slide down my cheek. The only one I'd cried that day.

"I know, darling. But, Casey, there's something else."

"Of course there is."

"Casey."

"Just tell me." I dropped my head into my hands.

"Sidetracks."

"Sidetracks?" I said into my lap.

"Your father never sold it."

I sat up. "Yes, he did. He sold it after the…after Mike."

"That's what I thought too, but apparently he's held onto the property for all these years, even the taxes are current. That cabin is yours now, Casey."

Jesus Christ, Sidetracks? I'd spent every summer of my childhood at Lake Kagachante. It was a warm, happy, place; a place where I had made a best friend…and lost him. Micah – Mike to me – had been the closet thing I'd had to a brother for 10 years. Mom had told me that after Mike's death Dad had sold the cabin – and now I hear that hadn't happened. So why did she tell me it had?

Okay. So Sidetracks instead of home. "Do you think I should go up there for the summer? I can't go back to school, yet. I just can't."

"I think it's certainly an option." Aunt Evie nodded. "We'll have to track down the key and maybe clean it up a bit – I imagine it's been awhile since anyone has been up there – but if that's where you feel you need to be, then that is where you should go."

I thought of the shimmering lake and the sounds of hummingbirds and children's laughter competing for supremacy; the creaky wooden floors of the cabin and the fresh breeze teasing the curtains in the evening. What had happened to Mike back then was sad, but it was a long time ago and I couldn't deny the elemental pull I felt toward the lake. Yes, Kagachante was where I needed to be.

*

As we turned onto the familiar dirt road that led down to the cabin I noticed a familiar, wooden building standing at the cross roads.

"That's Last Call!" I said excitedly.

"What's that?" Aunt Evie barely spared a glance for the old dive on the corner.

"It's a bar. My parents used to go there *all* the time with the Metz's. Mike's older sister would babysit and she always let us stay up super late. You never went with them?"

Evie arched a delicate eyebrow. "No. Your parents have always had unique tastes. That place looks like it should be condemned. Was it much nicer back then?"

"Eh…no, not really."

"Casey, you're not honestly thinking of going there?"

"Why not?" I shrugged. "It's walking distance."

"Casey, we're still miles away from the cabin. You could get assaulted out here."

I rolled my eyes so hard I almost dislodged them from their sockets. Evie was well meaning but the woman was so out of touch with the world. If I could survive a university campus for 3 years, a well-traveled dirt road would be a cakewalk.

The cabin had been my grandparents before it was my dad's. Aunt Evie had been out here hundreds of times when she was a kid but she seemed to have forgotten everything about the lake except how to get there.

As the last pale light of day fell into the horizon Evie's Mercedes crawled out into the open arena of the forest-encased lake. In the welling darkness the water appeared in front of us as a black void. The effect made it look like we were creeping toward a giant hole in the ground.

The other cabins around the lake were quiet and dark but I recognized them all and knew their family's names by heart. Only the Metz's cabin was lit and I choked a little as the breath caught in my throat. It had never even occurred to me that Mike's family still came to Kagachante.

Evie worked her way around the lake and parked next our cabin. It was much smaller than I remembered and if it hadn't been for the sign over the door which read *Sidetracks* I might have thought us at the wrong building altogether.

We unpacked the car and Evie went upstairs to put new sheets on the beds. I sat down on the long wooden bench beneath the kitchen window and laid my chin on my arms, staring out at the lake whose waves lapped eagerly at the grassy shoreline. I closed my eyes and inhaled deeply, hoping to breathe in some of the peace of the night.

After nodding off twice at the window I went upstairs to find a bedroom to sleep in. I smiled when I saw that Evie had made up the small room that had been mine as a child. It was just as I remembered it - a sturdy twin bed facing a pair of white double closet doors. A long bookcase ran along the wall and the wallpaper was covered floor to ceiling with pictures I'd drawn on it as a child. My parents had let me absolutely destroy those walls with crayon drawings; warm memories of the cabin and fun things I'd experienced there. I bent down to get a closer look.

There were simple drawings of my dad and I relaxing in the rowboat under a yellow son, pictures of the time we'd gone horseback riding, and a large, green drawing of my parents and I sitting at the fire pit making s'mores. I felt like a mace had hit me square in the chest.

I turned away from the happy pictures of a lifetime ago and collapsed onto the bed, wondering if I should move bedrooms to spare myself from the unwelcome pain I was suddenly feeling. I was asleep before it mattered.

*

"Are you sure you're going to be alright by yourself? I really hate the idea of leaving you here without a car, Casey."

I waved my hand at Evie while I took a sip from the coffee mug she'd handed me.

"If you need anything just call…"

"If I need anything I'll ask the neighbors. Don't worry about me, Evie, seriously."

"I'm coming to get you on the 29th. See if you can have a landline hooked up while you're here. Cell service is pretty spotty."

"It's fine, really. I kinda like being off the grid."

"Alright." Aunt Evie regarded me across the table and her expression sank into a sad, pitying look. I leaned back a little in my chair and looked out the window. Emotions always made me uncomfortable.

Evie noticed and stood up. "I have to get going. I promised to be back in St. Paul in time for a lunch meeting. I really hate to leave you this early."

"Go, go," I smiled at her and stood up. "How much trouble can I really get into around here?"

Evie laughed. "When you were a child: plenty. All you kids used to run around pulling pranks and tormenting the poor people down at Bay Lake."

"Pfft," I scoffed. "Bay Lake." *Those assholes.*

"Listen, I've put the groceries away and I was up early doing some of the cleaning. The water's on and I put your suitcases in the basement. Food is in the cupboards and I…I…"

Evie yanked me into a sudden hug and coffee went splashing over the rim of my mug. I held it out away from us so it wouldn't drip on her suit, making the hug all the more awkward.

"I'll be back soon." She said pulling away.

"Okay. Thanks for everything, Evie."

She patted my head and then grabbed her roller board and disappeared out the front door. I stood there in that awkward position until I heard her car turn onto the dirt road back toward town.

I sat back down in the wooden booth and drummed my fingers on the table. What now? It was too early to drink so…cigarette?

I walked out onto the patio and sat on the wrap-around bench that faced the lake. I curled my knees up to my chest and lit a Marlboro Light. Nothing like a little fresh air, right?

It was still early and the lake was covered in a heavy, gray mist. All was silent except for the gentle lapping of the waves on the dock. It was peaceful here. I closed my eyes and tried to remember weeks I'd spent here over the years. Catching frogs, barbequing, taking the boat out with my dad, racing Mike around the lake… the memories turned on me so fast.

Mike was chasing me down the dock with a sparkler, his dad was yelling at him and I was laughing – but then the laughter turned to screaming and Mike was drowning, disappearing underneath the surface as if being dragged down. And then the vision changed and I was drowning too, feeling his pain, his fear…I couldn't open my eyes and I couldn't escape it.

The sudden whirling of a power tool lit up the morning's silence and something shattered at my feet. I looked down at the mug which now lay in pieces on the deck. I swore loudly and threw my cigarette into an old coffee can. The whirling was coming from the Metz's house where it sounded like someone was ripping the place apart inside. Maybe it wasn't Jarod and Lanie after all.

I spent the rest of the day reading, cleaning, and waiting for the excited screams of the neighbor kids as they spilled out of their cabins. But the lake was still quiet when noon rolled around and I began to wonder. Maybe everyone had had a late night the day before? I decided to go for a stroll and see.

The walk around the lake was about 6 miles. By the

time I was close enough to see Sidetracks again the shadows were long and the sun was behind the trees. I hadn't seen a single person, or even a car, on my adventure around the lake. Other than me, and whoever was destroying the Metz's cabin, Kagachante was deserted.

Mike's cabin was the last before mine and I tried to be as quiet as possible as I walked past it on the off chance that it *was* the Metz's in residence. The guilt I still lived with about Mike's death - and the thought of breaking the news of my parents to them - kept a wide berth between us.

As I came around the corner toward home, something caught my eye – a giant, dirty, green pickup truck with Georgia license plates parked on the side of the cabin. I couldn't imagine that it belonged to the reserved and proper Metz's. I breathed a little sigh of relief and headed up the gently sloping hill toward Sidetracks.

*

The next day was much the same as the first – cold and quiet. I read for a while in the morning and then pulled my phone out to play Angry Birds. My battery was down to 18% percent before noon and I had to venture into the basement to grab a charger out of my suitcase.

I had never been allowed in the basement as a kid and still felt uncomfortable at the thought of going down there. I had no idea why Evie felt the need to put my bags in the basement but I guess that was just Evie – hide the mess, keep up appearances. I opened the basement door and felt along the wall for a light switch. Of course it was at the bottom of the stairs. In the little sunlight I'd brought with me I could see that the stairs went halfway down and then turned right at a landing. My suitcases were sitting at the bottom. The room was dark and mostly empty except for a few buckets and tools set against the wall. I grabbed my charger and ran back up the stairs, shutting the basement door behind me. I spent most of that night drinking Arbor Mist, watching Game of Thrones on my laptop, and trying to text Nicole.

The next day was quiet and boring as well, except for the interment sounds of someone working next door. The less I found to distract myself with, the harder the grief tugged at me like a two year old begging for attention. It was the perfect day to try out my parent's old haunt so I waited until the sun went down and then dressed in jeans and a hoodie and started down the road toward Last Call.

The walk turned out to be almost 3 miles and the moon was out by the time I darkened the door of the bar. Several people turned to look at me as the door closed behind me and I quickly realized that this crowd was a bit rougher than I'd expected. I pulled my hood up over my hair and sat down at the bar.

After a few minutes the bartender came over to stand in front of me, but he didn't say a word.

"Hi, ah…what do you have on tap?"

"Budweiser. Bud Light. Coors." He clipped.

I leaned over the bar to see the fridge of bottled beer behind him. "Yeah, I'll take a…Blue Moon I guess."

He nodded at me and served my beer without the customary, useless orange I was used to.

I turned in my seat to look around the dive and tried to imagine my parents here: sitting at a booth, laughing with the Metz's, avoiding eye contact with the surly bartender…

I smiled at the thought and took a sip of my beer. When I lowered the bottle I realized I was attracting some uncomfortable stares so I turned back around and pulled out my phone. I wanted to try and text Nicole since I was in town but the service here was almost worse than it was at the lake. I messed around with my settings for a few minutes before I pulled up Angry Birds. I was getting aggravated those arrogant, green bastards.

"Are you texting your boyfriend, beautiful?" A voice said beside me.

"No. Angry Birds." I said without looking up.

"Mmm. Does your boyfriend know you're out at the bar all alone?"

"I'm not alone."

"Of course you're not, you've got me. You wanna come sit at my table? Or maybe on my lap?" He purred in a raspy voice and leaned further into my personal space.

I released my last bird – a Qui-Gon Jinn that I lunched at an imperial tower. The structure shuddered for a few seconds but refused to topple over on the Imperial Bacon. Qui-Gon was not a good bird for a structure attack, it was a rookie mistake, I was better than that. I flexed my fist against the bar and tried not to slam it down. This game was infuriating.

"Well, honey?"

"No, thanks." I said and pushed *Restart Level*.

"What'd you say, girl?" His voice descended to a lower, more threatening octave.

"Well, like I said I'm playing Angry Birds."

"Honey, I'm a lot more fun than Angry Birds."

"I don't think you understand: this *Star Wars* Angry Birds."

"You think I give a shit?" He moved in until I was forced to lean back and look up at him. I really should have been paying attention. He was a lot bigger than I'd estimated and looking around I realized I'd unknowingly been taunting the biggest, rapiest guy in the bar. *Holy Kenobi.*

"Eh…" I started.

"AJ, I'm surprised to see you here. Thought Marissa still had a restraining order on you." A new voice said from behind me and I turned to see a man leaning against the bar on my other side facing 'AJ'.

"Marissa's here?" The man croaked and stepped back from me.

"Oh, yeah, she's out on the patio with Rick Clime," he said casually. "I'm no expert but I don't think there's anywhere in this bar you can get away with 300 feet." The new guy's accent was thickly southern and he didn't bother to spare a look for me as he sipped from a whiskey glass.

"Shit, man, you can't let a bitch chase you out of your own bar."

"Another pearl of wisdom, thank you for sharing it with me. Hey, aren't you still on parole?"

"Man, fuck you, Rhodes." AJ threw a $10 bill on the bar and then walked out the front door, slamming it behind him.

I kept my eyes on the front door in case he came back and addressed the man beside me. "I suppose you're going to tell me I shouldn't be in here alone."

The man laughed. "I'm not gonna tell *you* anything."

My eyes snapped back to him and he winked. I gave him a slight but cautious smile. The man sat down at the bar and ordered another Whiskey Sour from the bartender, who'd been watching the entire episode with inappropriate amusement.

Should I buy his drink? Is that what people do in this situation? Do I introduce myself? Make small talk? Whiskey Sour looked a decade older than me. *Was that weird? Was I being weird?*

As I was mulling it all over he picked up his drink, paid for it, and then left the bar to return to a pool game he'd apparently been in the middle of playing.

I looked down at the grinning pig on my phone. "Stop smiling, you smug bastard." I muttered and clicked off the screen. Maybe that was enough excitement for one night. I asked for the tab while I finished my beer.

As I walked out to head back to the cabin I slid a quick glance at Whiskey Sour who was still playing pool at the back of the bar. He was leaning on a pool stick watching me; an amused smile pulling at the corner of his mouth. Two men were talking to him but he tracked me walk all the way to the door, not bothering to be discreet with his gaze. I gave him an awkward nod before pushing out into the cold air.

The walk home felt much longer — and colder — than the walk out had been. What should be a soft, summer breeze felt more like a late winter wind — yanking at my clothes and nipping at my exposed skin. When I turned the last corner before the lake I suddenly felt like I was in a very foreign place. The road seemed unfamiliar and the lake again looked more like a gaping, black hole than a body of water.

I finally entered the circle of cabins around Kagachante and walked along the shoreline, thinking it odd that the wind was whipping around the lake like a cat trapped in a paper bag but the water was as flat and still as a pane of glass. Well. Lake Kagachante was nothing if not odd.

I hurried along faster, eager to get inside the safe, sturdy walls of Sidetracks. I unlocked the door, pushed it open, and went straight for the fireplace. It was odd to think I was about to light a fire in the middle of June in Minnesota but Holy Kenobi, was it cold. I built a small stack of kindling like my father had taught me and then topped it with a few Firestarter logs that Evie had bought from the store.

I spent 20 minutes trying to light it before giving up in frustration. The wind was snaking down the chimney from outside making an unholy whistling and I didn't feel like fighting it.

I walked toward the kitchen to retrieve my phone charger and suddenly found myself face up on the floor staring at the ceiling. *Ouch.* I sat up and rubbed the back of my head. I couldn't possibly be drunk after four beers and half a bottle of Arbor Mist. Well…*maybe.*

My groan turned into a pathetic laugh. "You're a fucking *idiot.*" I said to myself.

And then I heard someone else laughing. It sounded like a child's giggle, but I had no idea where it came from. I braced my hands on the floor to stand up and realized I was sitting in a small puddle of water.

"What the hell?"

As I tried to deduce how exactly it had gotten there I noticed the basement door was wide open, too. I walked over to close it. The giggle must have been the wind in the chimney but…the water and the open door? I decided that was a mystery for tomorrow.

I doggedly climbed the stairs and fell into my bed. I

was happy to see the closet door in my room was still closed tight. I'd never been able to sleep when it was open. I stripped down to my underwear and pulled the covers over me, burying myself into a cocoon. Then I groaned.

I could tell by the sound of crickets and toads that my window was still open. I knew it would only be a few hours before I woke up frozen but I was too tired to do anything about it now. I rolled over and stared at a drawing on my wall that I'd done as a child. It was a picture of my dad and I fishing off the end of the dock. My last thought before sleep claimed me was how silly that was - everyone knew there was nothing alive in the lake.

*

Trying to draw the likeness of Kagachante was an exercise in migraines. Each way sketched it the lake always ended up looking as it had the night before – a scary black hole sunken into the earth.

I looked down at the drawing I'd just penciled and then back up at the lake. My picture was identical to what my eyes were seeing but there must be some minute detail that I'd added or missed which made the lake look so much more ominous on paper.

I leaned back against one of the tiki torches that lined my dock and picked up the coffee mug sitting next to me. Perhaps my heart just wasn't in it today.

As I watched the rippling blue waves splash against the end of the dock I considered that maybe it was *me*. Maybe this was just the way I saw the lake in my head. My emotions could be influencing my sketch, making the lake look more sinister and threatening than it was in real life.

I suppose that made sense. Mike had drowned only ten feet off the end of the dock I was sitting on. I took a sip of overly sweetened coffee and leaned my head back against the pole. I idly wondered if they had ever recovered his body or if I was even now sitting a few yards above his remains. I'd been too young at the time to be told and too afraid to ask.

An uninvited memory began to pull at the strings of my conscience: a hot summer morning and two kids throwing sticks at dragonflies while their parents drank Bloody Marys on a nearby deck. It was the end of a long summer and everyone under the age of 21 had run out of things to do.

"I'm so *bored*." I'd said to Mike. "There is *nothing* to do today."

"We can go to Bay Lake."

"They said they'd call the cops next time they saw us."

"We can take the rowboat out?" He tried.

"My dad won't let me unless there's an adult with us." I frowned.

"Okay…turtle hunting?"

"I'm not allowed to because of the one that bit me last year."

"Dang, Casey, well, what *are* you allowed to do?"

"Nothing." I whined and glanced back at the deck where our parents were drinking and paying us no mind. "They're not really watching us, though, are they?"

"No," Mike laughed. "They're not watching us at all. They probably won't even remember we're here until dinner time."

"So…let's do something we're not allowed to do." I said, rubbing my hands together like a villain in a cheesy movie.

"Like what?"

"Like...let's go swimming," I said.

"You said we can't go back to Bay Lake."

"Not there. *Here.*"

We weren't allowed in the lake – ever. The water was always so cold that our parents were certain we'd get hypothermia if we put one toe in it so when we wanted to swim they hiked us down to Bay Lake nearby. *Nobody* swam in Lake Kagachante.

Mike frowned. "Very funny, Case. It's too cold."

"Don't be such a baby." I said.

"I'm not!"

"Can't you swim?"

"Yeah, of course!"

"Then why won't you go in with me? We could do it real quick. Like two minutes." I said kicking off my shoes.

"It's not a good idea."

"So what?"

"I don't..." Mike watched me pull off my socks with unease. "Okay, two minutes only and we stay near the shore. Like right there next to that tall grass. That way our parents won't see us either."

"No way, it's not even deep there. Look, they're going inside anyway. Quick, let's jump off the end of dock!"

He paled. "We don't know how deep that is!"

"You said you could swim."

"I can swim! Fine, let's just go." Mike tore the sneakers off of his feet and threw them up the hill. I followed him down to the dock to the edge and looked over. The tide was in so the water was high.

"Well?" I said.

"You first," Mike crossed his arms and smiled at me. He thought I was going to back down. I wasn't.

"Fine," I said haughtily. "Out of my way, Rebel Scum." I took a few steps back and made a running jump off the end of the dock. As soon as I hit the water I knew I'd made a terrible mistake.

The lake was so cold it seemed to push in on me like a vice. I felt my fingers begin to numb immediately and thought of all the times I'd been sprayed with lake water in the boat and how it always had made me shiver in the hot sun. This had been criminally stupid.

I struggled to the surface in a panic, gasping in chill and then in pain. As soon as I'd drawn warm air into my lungs I turned back toward the dock to warn Mike but he was already sailing over my head.

He went in cannonball position and breached the surface a moment later, the same panic and agony carved on his own face.

"Swim for it!" I yelled at him through violently chattering teeth. I turned back toward the shore praying I'd reach the dock before the blood froze in my arms and legs. It was seven feet away. Five. I could hear Mike behind me. He was an excellent swimmer, turned out, strong and fast. I felt him closing in on me, about to overtake me. But he never did.

The rest of that day was fractured to me; a blur of screaming, crying, sirens, and flashing lights. I remember all the neighbor kids looking at me in horror. And the quiet murmurs of the adults as they slid glances at me through guarded, distrustful eyes. *It wasn't my fault!*

But I knew better now. It was my fault. I shook free of the memory and reached up to rub some warmth into my cold face. Something stabbed my cheek and I realized I was still holding my pencil.

I looked down at my sketch pad and realized I'd been idly drawing while playing hostage to the past. In my sketch, a few feet off the end of the dock, I'd drawn a small hand reaching up out of the water. But that wasn't what made me gasp.

In the background a very tall, skinny figure stood alone and watched the drowning from where he stood on the opposite side of the lake. It had been drawn as a simple, black figure with hardly any detail. I kicked the sketchbook away from me and watched it slide across the dock toward the water. It teetered on the edge but didn't fall in.

"Hey, Angry Birds." My head snapped up to find Whiskey Sour striding down the dock. *You've got to be kidding me.*

I arched an eyebrow to hide my surprise. He was wearing jeans, a Metallica shirt, and a ridiculous black cowboy hat to compliment his deep, southern accent. As he walked he pulled out a pack of cigarettes, yanked one out with his teeth, and lit it with a zippo that was there and gone so fast all I could hardly be sure I saw it at all.

"Jesus Christ," I said looking him over. "Who let you north of the Mason-Dixon Line?"

"Oh, you like the hat?"

"I didn't say that."

"Angry Birds, you wound me," he laughed. I liked the sound.

"Oh, please." I rolled my eyes. "So you're the one

tearing apart 205. You buy that cabin from the Metz's?'

"I did. Actually, 205 is the third property I've bought in this area. I have one down at Bay Lake and I flipped that one last year," he pointed at a cabin across the lake. "I tried to buy 203, too, but they weren't interested in selling."

"Hmm. Well, I might be." I said.

"Ah, so you're the new owner." He eyed me with new interest and took a drag off his cigarette.

"Yeah," I sighed. "That's me."

"Well, good luck selling if that's what you've a mind to do. 214 has been on the market for 10 months."

I laughed. "Perhaps you should have done some research before you bought anything on Kagachante."

"Oh, really. What don't I know?"

"Well for one this isn't your 'typical' recreational lake," I said drawing my knees up under me. "Surely you've noticed Kagachante is…different."

"Sure, I mean, it's quiet here and the lake is…it's…" I understood his hesitation. No one could ever really put their finger on it.

"It's odd," I said. "Have you noticed the tides?"

"They're difficult to miss." Whiskey Sour muttered as he flicked out his cigarette.

"Yeah, no kidding. I know a lot of lakes have negligible tides but this one is huge. I mean it's like a six foot drop."

"Yeah, it's a mystery. But I don't understand why that would keep people away."

"Because it's unnatural. And have you noticed how frigid the water is? In the dead of summer?"

"Yeah. But good for fishing," he shrugged.

"Yeah, you'd think but there aren't any fish in this lake, either." I said.

"So you can't swim and you can't fish. Goddamn, that's a hard sell." He rubbed the back of his neck in an uneasy gesture.

"When I was a kid my dad told me the Lakota in this area believed that the own Devil's heart beat at the bottom of the lake. And that's why it has tides."

Whiskey Sour raised an eyebrow at me. "The devil?"

"That's why the Lakota named the lake Kagachante: It means 'Demon's heart'."

"Of course." He said seriously but the corner of his mouth pulled back in a smile.

"Don't laugh, you're the guy who sunk thousands of dollars into this area."

"Well," he said, "at least I got to meet you. So I guess it's not a total loss."

"You don't even know my name."

"Well, mine's Jesse."

"Oh God, of course it is." I laughed. "I'm Casey."

"I like that. Casey."

"Glad you approve."

He propped an elbow on the tiki pole and took off his hat to wipe imaginary dust from it. "Listen, seeing as we're neighbors and all how about you come over for a barbeque tomorrow?"

"Hmm, I don't know. I'll have to check my schedule." I picked up my coffee mug and poured the cooled liquid into the lake.

"I'm a nice guy, Casey, what more do you want to

know about me?"

"Hmm." I put a finger to my face and tapped my chin. "What do I want to know about you... How old are you?"

"29."

"Where are you from?"

"Georgia."

"What's your middle name?"

"Devin."

"Your favorite color?"

He eyes flicked down my body. "Green."

I pretended that I was not aware I was entirely clothed in green.

"Favorite animal?"

"Beef."

I laughed. "A Georgia boy through and through." He tipped his hat at me. "Alright, you win. I'll see you tomorrow night. What should I bring?"

"Chicken."

"I don't have chicken. Or a car."

Jesse shrugged his shoulders. "Well, I guess you better get huntin' then."

I scoffed. "You want me to go chicken hunting."

He smiled at me as he pushed up off the pole, and then started down the dock toward shore.

"I mean, I've got some eggs." I called after him.

"I can't grill eggs, Casey." He said without turning around.

"Tin foil!" I yelled after him.

Jesse laughed as he started toward the Metz's cabin. *His* cabin. I watched him for a moment before I stood up and walked back up the hill toward Sidetracks. I felt the familiar fluttering of attraction and conquest stirring in my belly. This guy was either going to be the distraction I desperately needed or one I could not afford.

*

I rolled over and the pillow between my knees fell to the floor. Cursing, I opened my eyes a fraction to find the bedroom flooded with light. Morning. My oldest foe.

I reached down to retrieve the pillow from the floor, hoping for a few more minutes – or hours – of sleep. When I pulled it back up onto the bed I squealed as wetness immediately soak through the thin quilt covering my legs. "What the hell, come on." I said to the room.

I sat up and blinked several times to let my eyes adjust to the sun. I swung my feet to the floor and then quickly picked them up again. There was a puddle of water next to my bed – and it was *cold*.

I got up, more confused than ever, and found that the water trailed out of the bedroom and into the hallway. "Ugh, not again."

I wrapped the quilt around my shoulders and followed the puddles around the house. The water led down the hall, down the stairs and down into the basement – a door that had somehow creaked open again in the middle of the night.

I opened it wider and walked down to the landing, then said my first four letter word of the morning. The basement was flooding. My empty suitcases sat at the bottom of the stairs in several inches of water. I walked down and pulled them up onto the landing. It was just my luck, wasn't it? Own my first house – pipes burst before the ink is dry on the deed. I stomped back up the stairs and pillaged the hall closet for towels.

I spent the next hour mopping up water and trying to soak it out of the carpet in the upstairs hallway. I had no idea how the water had gotten up here. Maybe pipes were leaking under the wooden floor. Was that even possible? Or had the water been tracked in somehow? I thought maybe Whiskey Sour from next door would be a good person to ask. I decided to wait until that evening when I went over to his cabin.

I'd just hung the last towel on the window sill to dry when I heard a deafening slam from the first floor of the house. The only door I'd left open was the one to the basement so I wasn't surprised to find it shut when I went downstairs. Even though I wrote the culprit off as a draft from the open windows, I locked the basement door for the rest of the day.

I knew it was absurd, but I couldn't shake the feeling that I wasn't alone in the house any more.

*

"Here," I said as I handed Jesse the bottle of Macallan. "You can't grill Scotch either."

He smiled and stepped aside to invite me into 205. I'd been curious to see if the place looked the same as it had when the Metz's lived here but the cabin was absolutely gutted. Among the limited furnishings was a couch that sat alone in the living area and a kitchen consisting of nothing but a card table and three chairs. I peaked around the corner into the dining room and was surprised to see the wall had been knocked down between it and the back parlor. The smell of fresh cut wood and lacquer filled the air and heavy power tools lay on a tarp covered pool table.

"Where did you get this?" Jesse asked from where he was still standing at the door. "This is a '92!"

I shrugged. "I found it in the kitchen. My dad used to drink scotch."

"You dad has good taste." He said admiringly. I didn't correct his tense.

Jesse opened the bottle and poured with a reverence reserved for someone well acquainted with fine liquors. He offered me a glass and I took it skeptically. Scotch wasn't usually my thing.

Jesse drank slowly, pausing between each swallow in a pretentious way. I watched him for a minutes and then shook my head and downed my entire glass. There was no need to stand on ceremony here.

Jesse didn't seem to mind that I hadn't worshipped the Macallan as he had and nodded toward a few bottles of wine on the counter. One had already been uncorked and I carefully poured the velvety red into a wine glass. The scotch was already working its magic and I was felt relaxed and unguarded. It was the first time in weeks.

I picked up the glass and turned around to find Jesse watching me. He was leaning against the kitchen counter, one hand resting on the lip of the granite and the other swirling the scotch in his lowball glass. He was quietly watching me.

"So?" I asked bringing the wine glass to my lips. "Food?"

"Potatoes are already on the grill and steak is next," he said casually. "How do you like yours cooked?"

"Generally mashed but I'd settle for baked if that's

what you're doing."

A smile teased the corner of his mouth.

"Medium rare." I said.

"Good. I was afraid you were one of those 'well done' people."

"I like to think I'm more civilized than that."

"So you are. Would you like a tour?"

Seeing the house again had been a half the reason I'd agreed to come over. Seeing the hot neighbor had, of course, been the other half. But now that I was in a room with him, the house felt small and inconsequential. His presence was heavy…distracting…and intoxicating as hell. "Yeah, I should probably see the house," I said.

There wasn't actually much to see. The rest of the rooms in the house were empty except for one bedroom. The upstairs bathroom had been torn up and the carpet had been stripped out of Mike's old room.

"This was my friend's room when we were kids." I said. Jesse nodded. "I figured it was a kid's room. Lots of posters on the wall and kid's toys."

"They didn't take that stuff when they moved out?"

"Nope. The guy was more interested in the money. Seemed happy to unload the place."

That made sense.

After the tour I followed Jesse out front to the grill. As he threw the steaks on, I sat down cross-legged on the porch and leaned back again a wooden support to discreetly watch him while feigning interest in the sunset.

We chatted about where he was from and what I was studying. I didn't bring up my parents and tried to work around the subject. We sat outside on the deck while we ate even though there wasn't any furniture. Jesse noticed me shifting uncomfortably against the pillar.

"Yeah...I'm sorry about this. We can go inside if you want; I've got a card table in there."

"It's fine, really." I said. I set my plate on the ground next to me and picked up the glass of wine I'd brought outside. Jesse was sitting opposite me leaning against the other pillar, one leg hanging off the deck. The cowboy hat sat back on his head and his wrist was resting on a raised knee where he continued to swirl the scotch around in his glass.

"Thanks for the save last night, by the way." I finally said. Jesse smiled while he chewed on a piece of ice and tipped his hat at me.

"So, how long until you're done with this place?" I asked.

"Awhile. I've got a lot on order and it's just me working on the property so...maybe by the end of the year."

"So flipping houses is your full-time job, then."

"Pretty much," he shrugged. "I like doing it and it's profitable so I figure why not?"

I nodded down into my wine glass. "What were they like? The Metz's?"

"Well, I only met the guy selling the place. He was...interesting."

"I'll bet he was. His son died while they were here."

"I had no idea."

"No, I wouldn't think he'd talk about it much. Our

families are – were – pretty close. It was traumatic for them."

"I can't imagine."

"Do you have kids?" I hoped the question didn't sound as loaded as it was.

He shook his head. "Do you?"

"No. I don't even have parents anymore."

Jesse watched me, his expression unreadable.

I looked out toward the lake and took a long sip of wine. I realized that this was the first time I'd said it out loud.

"They died a few weeks ago in a boating accident. Both of them." My voice broke over the last word.

"Casey…"

"It sounds so stupid doesn't it?" I laughed mirthlessly and looked down at the white knuckled grip I had on the wine glass. "*Boating accident.*"

I didn't look up as Jesse set down his drink and stood. He walked over and sat down next to me, gently taking the glass out of my hands.

"I know you're wondering why I'm here by myself."

"No," he said.

"It's okay," I shrugged. "I guess this is how I mourn: alone in a cabin getting drunk on Arbor Mist." I frowned. "Ugh. So disgusting."

Jesse sighed. "I don't normally offer advice in situations like this. But, Casey, you really have to stop drinking Arbor Mist. Someone like you deserves Chateau Margeaux."

"I don't know what that is." I said.

"Neither do I."

I don't know why it happened; maybe it was the clever levity he'd brought to the moment, or just being near someone after I'd been so alone, or maybe it was even the booze. It was probably the booze. I turned toward him and leaned in but he was already there, reaching behind my head to tangle his fingers in my hair and kissing me like an old lover. He tasted like smoke and scotch and-

He broke away.

"What…why?" I asked through labored breaths. Jesse stood up and backed away to the other side of the deck, running both hands through his black hair.

"I'm sorry. I'm sorry, Casey, you're obviously emotionally vulnerable right now but you just look so…so…" He stopped and glanced back to where I was still sitting on the floor.

"'Emotionally vulnerable'?" I laughed. "I appreciate you don't really know me, but no one would ever call me that. Look, Jesse, we're both adults. This doesn't have to be a mess."

He watched me for a second as if weighing the truth of that. Then he picked up his glass from where he'd left it and took a deep swallow of the amber liquid.

I raised an eyebrow at him in question and he leaned back against the pillar, shoving one hand into his pocket. "I don't think I'd mind it if it was, Casey."

A shiver ran down my spine but I'd never felt so warm. This guy was something else. "Pool?"

Four hours later, Jesse and I had found a comfortable cadence with each other. I'd won two games and Jesse had won…well…I'd lost count. He didn't take it easy on me, which I appreciated, and he helped me line up my shots and gave me some good pointers.

But as the night wore on, the shots became more difficult and the positioning became more…intimate. I could feel his breath on my neck, his hands holding mine steady, his body leaning into the curve of mine as I bent over the pool table…it was a game much older than the one he was teaching me.

I'd long since switched over to the Scotch and as I poured myself another glass Jesse flipped through stations on an old radio that sat in the corner.

"Wait, stop!" I yelled. "Go back."

"Where? To this?" Jesse turned the dial back to Alannah Myles and her slow, throaty version of "Black Velvet". "Are you serious?"

"You don't like this song? You know it's about Elvis." I said pointing to the Elvis Presley shirt he was wearing.

"Really…" Jesse said as he watched me. I could never help but dance to this song and I knew full well how provocative it could be, *especially* with half a bottle of scotch lending me confidence.

"I'll bet I could make you like this song." I teased as I slowly pulled the hem of my shirt up over my hips, exposing the skin underneath.

"I'll bet you could." Jesse said thickly.

"And I have a bet for you," I said as I pushed Jesse down onto the couch and stepped back from him. "Look but don't touch."

Jesse took a long, slow sip of scotch without taking his eyes off of me and leaned back on the sofa. "I accept," he said and I gave him a sly smile.

I won my bet that night. Jesse lost his.

*

It took me a moment to orient myself the next morning. The windows were covered in purple heavy curtains that almost entirely blocked out the morning sun and the bed was warm.

Jesse lay next to me, one arm curved possessively over my hips. In a burst like a camera flash the previous night rushed back to me. Every. Last. Detail. I shuddered. Jesse, mistaking it for a shiver, pulled the heavy comforter over my hip as he continued to doze.

I was wary of the kind of awkward encounter I could expect when he woke up. I quietly climbed out of his bed and braced myself against the window sill, waiting for the pounding headache to plow into me like a freight truck but it never did. In fact…I felt great. I glanced at the empty bottle of Macallan on the nightstand. Whiskey – who knew?

I pulled on my pants and tiptoed downstairs to grab my shoes. As soon as I was clear of the house I ran barefoot across the expanse of dewy-wet grass between our cabins. As soon as I was safe on the other side of my front door I leaned back against it and smiled. Holy shit. Holy. Shit. I needed to call someone. *Anyone.*

I was halfway through the house before I started to notice the water on the floor. I must have really been in La-La Land because it was *everywhere*. Shit. I'd meant to ask Jesse about this before I got…distracted.

The water trailed through the kitchen, up the stairs, and into my bedroom again. And it ended – where else? – at the basement door. The *open* basement door.

Okay. Pipes could be leaking. Basement could be

flooding. But nothing could explain how a definitely locked door had somehow opened itself.

I jerked it open further as if I'd find the culprit standing right behind it. My stomach dropped to the floor when I saw how much the water had risen since yesterday – several feet. This was definitely a problem.

I mopped up all the water I could manage with the still-damp towels from yesterday and wrung them out in the bathtub. I re-draped them along the window sills before I took a shower with the only remaining dry towel in the house.

I dressed in yoga pants and a white tank top and lay in bed while I dialed Nicole's number. The line couldn't connect – no shocker there. I tried several more times with moderate success and finally left a garbled message for her to cringe over.

I rolled over and then tried Aunt Evie. The phone rang a little clearer this time and I traced my finger along the wall on a picture of Micah and me building a rock fort. I remembered that day. It was a fun day.

It was clear that the past was everywhere around this lake but I realized that the good memories more than out-weighed the bad ones. And last night had proved that good company could make the lake tolerable. *More* than tolerable.

I realized the phone had stopped ringing and pulled it away from my ear to see that it was sitting at the home screen. One thing was for sure: if I was going to stay out here I was going to get a landline.

It had by now been several hours since I'd left Jesse's house and the sun was high enough in the sky that I considered the doorbell fair game. He answered fairly quickly but it was obviously I'd woken him up.

"Shit. I woke you up."

He gave me a warm, slow smile and leaned against the door frame, crossing his arms in front of him. "Well, well, well. Casey Grace."

"Jesse Devin." I smirked.

"I hope you're here to come back to bed."

"Well, actually, I have a sort of situation."

The smile fell off his face and Jesse pushed himself off the door frame. "What kind of situation?"

"My basement is flooded. My pipes are leaking. And there's a ghost in my house leaving locked doors wide open like some sorta asshole."

Jesse arched an eyebrow. "I think I can help with two of those things."

*

After he looked over the entire house Jesse headed into the basement to check on the flooding. It didn't take him long to make a diagnosis.

"It's not your pipes, Casey."

"But then where is this water coming from?" I asked from where I stood on the landing.

"It's lake water."

"*Lake* water? How the hell is it getting in here? I'm uphill from the lake!"

Jesse looked over at me and tapped the wall with some sort of tool I'd never seen before. "You have a two foot hole in the wall of your basement. It's submerged right now but, believe, it's there."

"How does this explain the water upstairs?" I asked, incredulous.

"It doesn't."

"Well, what do I do?" I shivered. I should have known it was lake water. The temperature in the basement had dropped quite a few long, cold degrees.

"You do nothing. I'll need a buddy of mine to come up here but I can patch your wall at cost."

"That's really nice of you but I'm just a poor college student."

"Don't worry, I'll take care of it."

"A poor, orphaned college student."

Jesse laughed. "I'll take care of it, I'll take care of it."

I shrugged. "I'm just kidding. I have some money from my parent's life insurance. Can you ballpark the cost?"

Jesse shook his head as he started packing up his tools. "I said don't worry about it, Casey Grace."

"I can't let you do this job for free." I said. He gave me an unreadable look and then waded over, stepped up out of the water and peeled off the gators he'd been wearing. "Damn, you were not kidding. That water is frigid."

"I don't know if you've noticed but it's always that cold."

"Well, I can't imagine swimming in that."

I turned back up toward the stairs. "That's because you can't."

"No one's ever tried?"

"I'm sure they have but there was a drowning about 12 years ago." I tried to keep my voice as level as possible.

"Jesus. Did you know them?"

"Yeah, I did. Coffee?"

A few minutes later we were sitting out onto the deck. It was another cold, quiet, beautiful morning.

I took the seat facing the house while Jesse faced the lake. I pulled my hands inside my sleeves and cupped them around the hot mug of coffee.

"So." He said.

I sighed. "You want to know about the drowning."

"Only if you want to talk about it." Jesse leaned forward and rested his arms on the table.

I shrugged. "Maybe I should. This is actually my first trip back to the lake since the day Mike died." I set the mug down on the table and twisted it in my hands.

"Were you there when it happened?"

"Oh, yeah. The whole thing was actually my fault. We were bored, I suggested it…Mike went along with it because I basically called him a pussy for objecting. We jumped into the lake and-" I shrugged. "-he never came back out."

"I'm sorry, Casey. But you have to know that wasn't your fault. Kids-"

I gave him a dismissive wave. "It was years ago, I've accepted my role in it."

"Did you talk to anybody about this stuff? A therapist? That's a lot for a kid to deal with."

"No, we didn't even talk about it at my house. My parents acted weird around me for a long time. They seemed sorta wary of me for a couple years; like they didn't trust me, like I'd done it on purpose." I sighed. "I suffered nightmares. I saw myself drowning, I felt myself drowning. All the pain, and panic, and fear. It was awful."

I looked up at Jesse to gauge his reaction to all this. He was looking at me with a certain intensity, solemn and sad. But it wasn't pity, it was more like...

Something moved behind his head. My eyes snapped up to the second floor window and I saw a figure there. Small, and hard to make out in the darkened room, but definitely there.

I was out of my chair and through the door before Jesse caught the mug that had gone spinning off the table during my flight.

I ran up the stairs, taking them 3 at a time, and paused at the bedroom door. The figure I'd seen was no longer at the window but there was water everywhere. I ran to my closet and flung the doors open – but the room was empty. I called for Jesse as I went running out of the room and literally ran into him at the top of the staircase. He caught me before I went tumbling down.

"What's wrong?" He asked as he set me back on my feet.

"There's a fucking kid in here! I saw him in the window. That's what's happening, some kid is coming into my house and tracking all that water up from the basement!"

"What? Where would a kid-"

"Bay Lake! It's only a couple miles south through the woods. We always used to prank the cabins there and they would prank us. Like a friendly rivalry but WE DREW THE LINE AT BREAKING AND ENTERING." I yelled the last part, hoping the little shit would hear me.

"Alright, alright, I'll help you look."

We went room to room, calling to the kid, yelling that

wouldn't hurt them, promising we weren't mad. When the trail went cold back at the basement stairs I threw up my hands in frustration. "We were only outside for like ten minutes!"

"Yeah, this really doesn't make sense," Jesse shook his head. "I've been here since April and I haven't seen any kids in this area."

I shut the basement door and locked it again. "Bay Lake is really close. That's where we went swimming when we were kids."

Jesse frowned. "I think you should file a police report just to get something on the record."

"No," I shook my head. "It's just some kid. Pranks are a part of lake life, especially out here where there's nothing to do."

"Alright, well listen, I have to go into town today and order supplies to plug the hole in your basement. Are you sure you don't want to come and just *talk* to the cops?"

I sighed. "I'm sure. This is just a kid who doesn't understand boundaries."

Jesse nodded. "Keep your doors locked from now on, and your windows."

"Trust me, I will. Thanks for helping me."

"Casey Grace." Jesse murmured pulling me in close. "How dare you suggest that I would do otherwise?"

*

Jesse left the next morning to check out another property he was interested in near the Canadian border. I heard his truck pull in late that night and debated getting up and going to spend the night with him. God knows I wanted to.

I breathed a sigh of relief the next morning when I woke up to dry floors and a locked basement. I didn't bother to check on the flooding. The knowledge that Aunt Evie would be here in less than a week weighed on me with a new found gravity. For the first time in weeks I didn't feel empty or alone. And I wasn't ready to give that up.

There was no denying that there was a strong, almost innate, attraction between Jesse and I. I could blame it on the loneliness, or the emptiness, or the grief. But in the end, there it was. It was probably the type of thing that would burn bright and hot for a brief eternity and then explode in a thousand tiny embers of jealousy, anger and accusations. But still…what if?

What if, indeed. I spent all of Saturday trying to get Evie on the phone. I needed another week, a few more days, anything. I wasn't ready to go home and face all the pity and uncomfortable looks. I didn't want Evie showing up here, yet.

Jesse spent his Saturday in town checking on his Bay Lake property and picking up supplies for his upstairs bathroom. Since the inventory truck from Minneapolis wasn't getting in until late that evening I told him to just stop by the next morning.

I gave up on Evie around 7 and watched Game of Thrones - *Joffrey, you twat!* - on my laptop. There was no way around it: if I wanted to get ahold of my aunt, I'd have to go to town. I felt uncomfortable leaving the cabin while some little jackass ran around thinking it worth his time to come into my house uninvited, haul water up from my basement, and spill it up and down my hallways.

Even though Jesse still wasn't convinced I was being stalked, he kept an eye on my house when I was over at

205 with him. I could tell he was genuinely perplexed by the entire situation but seemed determined to end it.

I felt myself begin to nod off around 9 so I shut my laptop and set it on the bookcase. Before I got back in bed I went room to room double checking all the locks on the windows and doors – and triple checked the lock on the basement. When I was satisfied that nobody was getting in without breaking something heavy I stretched out on my bed and pulled the covers up to my chin. Even though I loved the sounds of the lake at night I wouldn't be opening my bedroom window that evening.

I let my eyes flutter shut but now that I was ready sleep wouldn't come. I flipped over and over – side, stomach, back – but nothing seemed to help. Something just didn't feel right. After a few frustrating hours I opened my eyes, resigned to the fact that there was more Game of Thrones in my immediate future. I sighed and rolled over to grab my laptop – and then realized what was bothering me.

The closet was cracked open. I'd forgotten how much I *hated* that fucking closet. I'd never been able to sleep when it was open. It made me feel unsafe. The black abyss behind the doors seemed deeper at night, as if the closet stretched for a dozen miles. And it didn't feel empty. It never felt empty.

It wasn't an unfamiliar fear, in fact it was almost nostalgic. As I laid there staring at void between the doors I remembered telling my dad years ago that a monster lived in my closet. A big, buck deer that walked on its hind legs and wore clothes and had a skull for a face. Dad always made sure the closet was shut after that.

I got up and closed the doors. They clicked softly shut and I gathered my pile of quilts and dragged them into my parent's room at the end of the hall. There would be no sleeping in my old bedroom tonight. Perhaps not again at all.

I flopped down onto their big, soft, queen bed and fell asleep almost immediately. It was unrestful. The closet haunted my dreams, spinning them into familiar nightmares. Something looked back at me from the abyss: the tall, thin, creature from my drawing. The thing wore black robes that were so long they piled on the floor at its feet. It chased me from room to room and then out to the dock and cornered me at the end. The child from the window waited in the lake, gentle waves distorting his face as he reached up out of the water.

I woke up completely out of breath. Any relief I would have felt to realize I was safe in bed was stifled by the unfortunate, familiar feeling of sleep paralysis. It didn't happen often, but I knew it well enough to recognize it, *thank god*. It can be a perfectly terrifying experience when you don't know what's happening.

As I waited for my body to catch up with my brain my eyes tried to focus on something in the room. They settled on the doorway which I slowly came to realize was filled with a person; the same little kid from the window that day, that had returned to me in a nightmare. So I was still asleep after all.

I studied the figure silhouetted against the moonlit hallway and thought I recognized him. I could make out enough of the kid to age him at about 9, maybe 10. There was something familiar about him and it nagged at me but I couldn't quite put my finger on what my brain was recognizing.

The child was watching me too, and had his hands

were cupped over his mouth as if to stop from making a noise. I waited for the nightmare to morph into a different scene as they so often did but as the seconds ticked by I began to feel control bleeding back into my body.

I was awake. *I was awake.* I screamed. The kid started laughing – a high pitched, giggling sequel I recognized from the night I tried to build the fire.

As I began to kick off the covers, the kid bolted from the doorway. I fell out of bed in a tangle of quilts and limbs. When I'd finally gained my feet, I looked around desperately for something to use as a weapon. After unsuccessfully trying to rip the curtain rods from the wall, I grabbed a bedside alarm clock and tore it from outlet.

I crept out of the room, avoiding the puddles of water that he'd left on the floor. I was no longer just annoyed with the little shit, I was downright angry, even a little scared. It was the middle of the night, what the fuck was he doing here?

I followed the trail of water along its familiar course to my bedroom and stepped inside. The water led not to the bed this time but instead trailed into the closet...which was cracked open...again. I finally had him. I thought of screaming for Jesse - he would probably hear me, he was a light sleeper. But he'd haul the kid off to the cops and I wanted to give him one last chance.

I dropped the alarm clock to my side and flipped on the light. I could tell before I got to it that the closet was empty. The kid had vanished and the floor inside was soaked in water. I wanted to scream.

I dropped the heavy clock onto the rug and rubbed my face, sliding down the wall to the floor.

"I can't keep this up," I whispered to myself. Nothing

made sense, I felt like I was going insane. I *knew* that kid, I was sure of it. But what 11 year old kid did I know this far north? Maybe 10 years ago, but not now.

I leaned my head back against the wall and turned it to the side, closing my eyes. I was so damn tired but there was no way I could sleep in this house anymore. That kid had to have broken a window to get it here. Jesse was right, I had to involve the cops.

I took a deep breath and opened my eyes. As I tried to muster the strength to stand, I noticed a loop of red crayon drawn behind the bookcase next to me. I'd never drawn anything behind the bookcase as a kid because it was too heavy for a 9 year old to move.

Curious, I sat up on my knees and with significant effort pulled the bookcase away from the wall. The picture behind it was large but simple. It was a dock, some crudely made waves, and two stick figures swimming in the water. One figure was swimming toward the dock and the other was below the waves. A third, impossibly tall stick figure was standing on the floor of the lake holding onto his ankle. The creature had a thin deer's face…and horns.

I hadn't drawn this. I didn't know who had drawn it but there was no way I was spending another second in the house with it. I stood up and calmly walked down the stairs, out of the house and right up to Jesse's door. 2AM or not, I considered this fucking nonsense an emergency.

I decided to knock instead of ring the bell at this hour, and a moment later Jesse opened the door.

"You know you don't have to knock, Casey Grace." He murmured in a thick accent that I was slowly beginning to appreciate.

"He's back. That kid."

Jesse's teasing, casual manner dropped as quickly as his smile. "Come inside." He said and led me into his living room, flipping on a nearby lamp. "Was he in the house?" He asked and picked up a baseball bat in the corner.

"Put that down."

Jesse raised his eyebrows. "Was he?"

"I woke up and he was just standing there watching me sleep."

"Where is he now?"

"I don't know. He ran and I couldn't catch him."

"You have to get the police involved, darlin'. You know that, right?"

"Yeah, I know."

"And Casey...look, I was going to tell you in the morning but...I went over to Bay Lake today to check on my other cabin. I spent the whole afternoon driving around and there's no one there."

"What? That's crazy. Bay Lake is always packed in the summer."

"Maybe a decade ago but not now. I spend several hours there and trust me, your stalker isn't coming from Bay Lake."

"But there's no one else here."

"I know. Maybe it's a kid from town."

"Maybe. But that's the other thing, Jesse, I found something else. There was this...picture on my wall. I used to draw on my walls all the time when I was a kid but I didn't draw this."

"A picture of what?"

"Of the day Mike died. It was a picture of us swimming

and a figure was holding onto him underneath the water."

"And you think this kid drew it?"

"Maybe. I mean, who else? I certainly didn't draw it." I hoped that was true.

Jesse crossed his arms and leaned back against the arm of his couch. "How would this kid even know about your friend Mike?"

"Well…look, I know this is going to sound fucking stupid but…that kid looked really familiar to me. I mean what if…what if it *is* Mike?"

Jesse stared at me. "You need a drink."

I sighed and rubbed the bridge of my nose. "Well, I can't argue with that."

Jesse disappeared into the kitchen and I threw my hands up in mortification, I was disgusted with myself. Had I really just accused a ghost of haunting me? This kid was really under my skin. I needed to rally the situation.

Jesse returned from the kitchen with a glass of wine in one hand and a whiskey in the other. I opted for the whiskey.

I took a long pull from the glass and when I lowered it I saw he was watching me again. In his face I saw serious concern but etched even deeper was hunger…and heat.

I'd forgotten that I had come straight to his house from bed. I chanced a glance down to find I was dressed in nothing but boy shorts and a white tank top.

"Sorry." I shrugged, taking another sip.

"I'm not." His eyes had yet to find my face.

"Look, Jesse, I know it sounds crazy but I really think something fucked up is going on in my house."

"Casey..."

"Okay, but what if it *is*, Mike. I mean, he'd have every right to be-"

"Casey, for the love of God, please."

"What?!"

Jesse walked over and wrapped his arms around me. I sagged a little in his embrace and tried to draw the strength out of him. God, I was tired. "Stranger things have happened. If you say it's your friend Mike, then maybe it is," he murmured into my hair.

I pushed him away and tried to read his face. "You don't really believe that." I said shaking my head.

"Yes, I do."

"No, you believe that *I* believe it."

"There's not much of a difference, Casey."

"There's a *world* of difference."

He sighed. "I just think that you've been through a lot lately – with your parents' death, the hole in your basement, and this kid messing with you. It-"

"I am *not* having breakdown."

"I didn't say that."

"Don't you think it's in the realm of possibilities that I'm right?"

Jesse rubbed his tired face. "Yes."

"But you don't think that's what's going on."

"No. Yes. Whatever you want." He ran a hand through his bed-messed hair. "I really can't concentrate when you're looking at me like that."

I realized the strap of my tank top had fallen off my

shoulder. *Fuck it, maybe I need the distraction.*

I set the whiskey down on the mantle next to me and peeled the tank top off over my head without hesitation. Jesse choked a little and I smiled at him and then picked the glass back up and downed the rest of the scotch – topless and freezing. *Worth it.* I thought as I watched the look that came over his face. And it was.

*

When I woke up the next morning I was alone. I could hear the muffled whirl of a rotary saw from downstairs and I smiled when I realized my tank top was still lying on the floor in the living room.

I pulled the covers up further to ward off the cool morning air and squeezed my eyes shut. Had I really suggested to Jesse last night that I was being harassed by a ghost? *Holy Kenobi.* The cringe was so strong I buried my face in the pillow next me. Perhaps it was best if I just snuck out this morning.

I found a pair of Jesse's flannel pajama pants in his dresser and pulled them on, then wrapped a thin, white sheet around my middle and quietly crept down the staircase. I snuck a look around the corner and saw that Jesse had laid my shirt on the back of his couch.

"Morning', Beautiful."

I turned around to find Jesse watching me from the kitchen; a coffee mug in his hand and an amused smile on his face.

"Eh…hi."

"Coffee?" He asked a little too smugly.

I smirked. "Yes, thank you." I raised my chin an inch and let the sheet drop to my feet while I reached out for the cup he offered me.

"My God," he said appreciatively.

"Oh please." I laughed and then walked into the living room to retrieve my shirt. Jesse seemed genuinely disappointed when I pulled it on.

"Listen, I've got about another hour's worth of work to do but after that I was hoping I could take you into town."

I sighed. "Yeah, that would be great. I really need to talk to my aunt."

"And I'd really like to talk to the police."

"You're right." I offered as I made my way toward the front door.

"And Casey – don't go back into your cabin until I've checked it out."

"Yes, yes, I get it. I'm just going to go sit on your dock."

Sidetracks held an ominous glow in the gentling rising light so I avoided looking at it. I made my way down to Jesse's dock and sat at the end letting my feet dangle over the water. The tide was out and the water was several feet below my toes. I thought about what I'd said the night before and tried to weigh if it held any water.

As much as I hated to admit it, the drawing behind the bookcase was consistent with my style. But I couldn't believe that I had drawn it. If it was the kid, how was he getting in? If there were no broken doors or windows it meant that he had a key – or that he had been in my house all along.

And if that were true than logic followed that he must be hiding out in the basement, coming up occasionally to wander the house and leave a trail of water behind him. But

I'd been in the basement: there was nothing down there and nowhere to hide. Okay…so that left the impossible. What if it was Mike? What did he want from me? Was he angry? Was he trying to warn me about something? I couldn't in a million years picture Mike trying to hurt me – even an angry, spiteful, dead Mike. We had been best friend friends. And what of the tall, deer-like creature I'd absentmindedly drawn on my sketchpad, and seen in my nightmares, and somehow remembered from my childhood? Nothing. Nothing made sense.

I could feel Jesse approaching before I heard him on the dock. He didn't say a word in greeting. I felt him kneel down behind me and entangle his hand in my hair, gently pulling my head back to him. He kissed me – soft, slow, lazy.

After he pulled away he sat down next to me and let one leg dangle off the dock while he rested his arm on the other. "I've been thinking about what you said."

"About what?" I asked.

"Your friend Mike."

"Ah. And?"

"If there's even a chance that you're right then you have to sell that cabin."

"I know."

"When are you leaving?"

I sighed. "My aunt should be here on the 29th."

"That's only four days away."

"I know."

There was a silence between that I couldn't bring myself to fill.

"I want to see you again, Casey."

I looked up at him and nodded. *God knows, so do I.*

"I can visit you at MSU."

"Anytime..." I began to feel an aching in my chest that I didn't care to explore. I decided to change the subject. "Can I shower before we go to town?"

"Definitely," Jesse brushed tiny pieces of wood off of his shirt. "I'm covered in saw dust."

"Great, will you give my house a once over so I can go shower and get dressed?"

Jesse didn't find any broken windows or broken doors, and the basement had remained locked for once. When he was satisfied that no one was in the house I promised I would only be ten minutes or so before closing the door with Jesse on the other side.

The water from the showerhead came out ice cold so I let it run for a full 5 minutes before I checked it again. It still wasn't at a tolerable degree. I swore out loud. My hair was thick and heavy and it took quite a while to wash. This was going to be an unpleasant experience.

I stepped into the tub and an inhuman hiss escaped my lips as the water sprayed down my back. "Now, I can't wait to sell this fucking cabin." I muttered.

I lathered soap into my hair as quickly as I could while taking measured breaths. After I'd rinsed the shampoo I smoothed on conditioner and scrubbed my body while hopping in and out of the stream of water.

Oh God, almost done. I had one foot out of the tub while I rinsed the conditioner out of my hair. This whole experience couldn't be over fast enough. I yelped as I felt the water drop a few degrees more.

As I yanked my fingers through my hair to make sure all the conditioner was out, a clump of it came loose in my hands. At first it was just a few strands but suddenly I was pulling away huge, oily chunks and screaming. I looked at my feet and found that the bathtub was filling with grey, murky water. With bittersweet relief I realized it wasn't hair I'd been pulling off my head – it was lake weed.

I hopped up on the edges of the tub and backed away from the showerhead, which had slowed to half-power as lake gunk backed up behind it. Holy shit - it *was* in my pipes!

I reached out with my foot and turned off the faucet, trying to avoid the trickle of the freezing cold demon water as much as possible. Stepping out of the shower I toweled off as quickly as I could.

After I was dressed, I decided to check the basement again on the way out of the house. The door was still closed and I unlocked and opened it with an unfounded caution, as if a deluge of water was waiting behind it to pour into the room like an elevator in the Overlook Hotel.

Daylight spilled down the staircase to catch upon the still, glassy water that had risen to just above the landing. I saw my suitcase floating across the room and groaned as I made a mental checklist of all the things in it that were ruined.

As watched it gently bump against the wall I noticed something stirring in the water. It was moving just beneath the surface and I was paralyzed as I watched it. Was it a fish? Some other type of animal? How the hell did it get in here?

It swam slowly under the water, and as it came closer to the staircase I noticed just how long it was – 12 feet, maybe more. *Holy Kenobi, it's a snake.*

It reached the landing and as I backed up a stair something thin and black broke the surface of the water, and reached up toward me. It looked like a bone and I backed up the stairs and slammed the door hard, trying not to scream. I took a few deep breaths.

"What do you want, Mike?" I asked the basement door. "What do you want from me?"

Silence.

"Please leave me alone. I'm, sorry. I'm so sorry. Please, Mike, this is my house, you have to go back to the lake."

Nothing. I leaned my ear against the door.

"Micah?"

But the only sound was the splashing of water on the walls and the desperate, terror-stricken gurgle of someone drowning on the other side.

I leaned my forehead against the door. There was finally silence on the other side. "Mike, please stop... I'm so, so sorry, I- I should never have made you go in the water. It's my fault, okay? It's all my fault." I was crying. I couldn't fathom how this was happening to me, or really how it was happening at all. "Please, go back to the lake, Mike..." I whispered through the door. "Please."

Suddenly a new sound sliced through the cabin - the voice of MC Chris. My phone was working; the only problem was that the sound was coming from the other side of the basement door.

It was impossible. I dropped to the floor and peeked under the door to see if I could see anything. The light was now on in the basement, another mystery since the light switch was at the bottom of the stairs, under four feet of water. The ringing suddenly stopped as the phone sent the caller to voicemail and I tore the door open to grab the android.

It was there, as casual as ever, sitting on the step just above the waterline. I moved cautiously down the stairs, looking for any sign of movement underneath the water's surface. I reached the step above the phone and snatched it from its place as quickly as I could. I ran halfway back up the staircase before I heard the sound of stirring water behind me and turned around.

Someone was crawling up the staircase behind me: slowly, step by step he reached out with the thin, black bones of his hands and I watched as his back broke the surface. His head was tucked down beneath the water and I didn't wait to see any more of it.

I slammed the basement door and backed up to the wall, eyes darting around for something heavy to push in front of the basement. Just as I spotted my dad's old chair the sound of something scratching along the floor reached my ears. My eyes were drawn to the basement door again where something long and spindly was coming through the crack at the bottom. The thin, black fingers curled upward on the door as if to rip it from its hinges.

I dropped the phone and shot out of the house like a bullet. I was screaming loud enough for Jesse to hear me and I hit the steps of his front patio at a dead run. He opened the door as I cleared them and caught me while I screamed at him, hysterical and shaking.

"Casey, slow down!"

"I was wrong. I was so wrong, Jesse, he hates me. He wants to kill me. Please get me out of here. Please Jesse."

"Alright, okay, we'll leave. Come inside, let me grab my

keys." I followed him into the kitchen, absently rambling the entire way. "He's angry that I killed him. He's coming in from the lake, he was coming up the basement stairs, Jesse, he's going to kill me, I can feel it. He wants to pull me into the lake and drown me."

Jesse stopped and turned around to say something but when he saw how badly I was shaking, he wrapped his arms around me instead. "Just breathe," he whispered into my hair. "Just breathe, Casey."

And I tried. But my heart was going a million miles a minute and it needed the oxygen desperately. I reached for a nearby whisky with shaking hands. Jesse saw what I was after and took the bottle from me. I leaned back against the counter and tried to figure out how to put what had happened in the basement into words. As I rested my hands on the counter behind me to brace myself I felt a few sheets of paper shift under my palm and flutter to the floor. I leaned down to pick them up.

"Let me." Jesse said.

I turned around to straighten the remaining stack and a name on the top sheet caught my eye. I grabbed it off the counter and re-read it, confident that I'd read it wrong the first time.

"Why does this have Mike's name on it?"

"What?" Jesse asked.

"Micah Metz. Why does this paper say Micah Metz?" I asked.

"He's the guy who sold me this house. Bit of an asshole, honestly."

"That's not possible." I breathed.

"Casey, I know you're a family friend but this kid was

total jackass."

"No," I squeezed my eyes shut and shook my head. "No, Micah died when he was a kid, Jesse, I told you that."

"Micah Metz…is your friend Mike?"

"There's no way he sold you this house."

"Casey…" Jesse gently pulled the paper out of my shaking hands.

"Mike has been dead for over a decade."

"Then this isn't the same guy. This kid is alive, he drives a mustang…he's your age."

"You're lying."

"I would never lie to you."

"Who are you?"

Jesse reached out to gently grab my wrist. "Casey."

The ringing of my phone sliced through the clearing and cut the tension between us like a hot knife. I jerked my wrist out of Jesse's grasp and ran out of his house.

"Casey!" Jesse yelled after me. I didn't know if he followed me - all I could focus on was the sound of my cell phone and help on the other end of it. *Please be Evie. Please be Evie.*

I snatched my phone from where I had dropped it in the hallway. Evie's name was on the screen.

"Hello? Evie? Hello?"

"Casey? Sweetheart, what's wrong? I have a dozen missed calls from you and every time I call back I'm sent straight to voicemail."

"Aunt Evie, listen. I need to ask you something. Do you remember my friend, Micah Metz? From the lake?"

"Of course, his family owned the cabin next door. Why? Are they there?"

"No, no, 205 actually belongs to someone else now." My eyes flicked to door. Jesse was there, leaning against the door jamb with his arms folded in front of him. He watched me through cautious, worried eyes.

"Alright. Casey, what is it?"

"Evie, do you remember the day Mike died? You and Mom and Dad were inside with the Metz's and Mike and I jumped in the lake. Do you remember that?"

"Casey, do *you* remember that?"

"Of course! Why wouldn't I?"

"Sweetheart…what's brought this all on?"

"I think Mike is…still here. I think he blames me for what happened. I think…I think he's trying to hurt me."

"Casey, that's impossible."

"I know, but I can't explain it any other way. I can feel it, Evie. I saw him."

"Sweetheart-"

"He blames me for the way he died. He-"

"Casey! Casey…please calm down, I'm packing an overnight bag now. You're not being haunted by a ghost."

"I know how it sounds but Mike-"

"Casey…" Evie paused on the other end of the line. "Micah Metz isn't dead."

"But I remember-"

"Casey, it wasn't Micah that drowned in the lake that day - it was you."

I clutched the phone tighter to my ear. "What?"

"Sweetie, Micah was fine. He came tearing into the kitchen screaming that you went under. We ran out to the dock, your father and Jarod dove in to find you but...they couldn't. Your mother was hysterical, I called 911. It was terrible."

"I'm still alive..." I whispered.

"Yes. Because just as the divers were suiting up to recover your body you just sort of...walked out of the lake."

I shook my head and looked up at Jesse, confident he was hearing every word.

"It had been three hours since you'd gone under the water and you walked out of it with only a bad case of hypothermia. Your skin was pruned, your eyes were bloodshot, but you were breathing. They took you to the hospital and the doctors couldn't figure it out. You didn't speak for months. Your parents decided not to mention the incident until you were ready to talk about it. It sounds like you finally are."

"Why don't I remember."

"You remember what your mind can handle, Casey."

"I have to go Aunt Evie." I let the phone slide out of my fingers to the floor.

"Jesse." I looked at him.

"I know," he said quietly.

"I don't understand."

"Casey-"

"If it wasn't Mike crawling out of the basement, who was?"

Before he could respond something knocked on the

basement door.

"Don't open it," I whispered.

"Casey, get out of the cabin."

Jesse grabbed a fire poker and walked out into the hallway to stand in front of the basement door. He opened it slowly, weapon raised over his head. But there was nothing there.

"Listen, asshole." He shouted down the stairs. "You are trespassing and I'm beyond exhausted of your shit. Show yourself or I will beat the ever-living shit out of you." It was the first time I'd ever seen Jesse angry.

"Jesse," I pulled on his arm. "Let's go."

"Get out of here, Casey." He said quietly.

"I'm not leaving you here. This thing-"

Jesse turned around to look at me. "I'm going to handle this but I need you to get out of here."

"No, please, let's go."

"Casey, go back to my house and wait. There's-"

"Jesse, get away from the door."

"What?"

The water behind him had begun to stir. "Jesse, please, it's coming back!"

He spun around and watched as a swell of water moved toward us, the thing underneath barely concealed by a thin layer of water cresting its back. "What the hell?"

"Jesse!" I screamed, but it was too late. The thin, black arm shot up out of the water and grabbed onto Jesse's leg. He came down hard on the staircase and the creature pulled him down the stairs into the water. He was yelling at me but I didn't know what he was saying.

"Jesse!" I screamed over him and ran down the few steps to where he was already halfway submerged. I grabbed his arm and began to pull but he pushed me away, back up the staircase. "Go," he screamed.

"No! I-"

"Case-" and then he was dragged under the dark water.

"Jesse!" I screamed. "Jesse!"

He had to come back up. "Please, Jesse." I sobbed.

I thrust my hand into the water, searching for anything, any sign of him. I went down one step and reached further down the stairs. "Please don't leave me alone." I whispered as tears fell into the grey-brown abyss beneath me.

Something grabbed onto my hand and suddenly Jesse was there, crawling out of the water. I backed up all the way to the top of the stairs and screamed at him to hurry. He struggled to stand and I saw what it had done to him. His chest was ripped open, exposing the muscle and ribs underneath. One of his arms fell limply at his side, an open fracture protruding from his shoulder blade. Jesse started to pull himself up stair by stair, but as he dragged himself, flesh tore off his chest in ribbons. I ran down to help him.

"No!" He screamed. "No."

Suddenly he stopped climbing and reached down to pull something out of his pocket, and then threw it up the stairs at me. I watched his car keys hit the wall opposite the basement door and turned back to look down at Jesse, who was now lying perfectly still.

"I'm sorry," he whispered before he was suddenly jerked underneath the water again, as if he'd never been there at all.

"No! Jesse, no!" I threw myself down the stairs and

waded as far in as possible before I had to start swimming. I'd only been in the water mere moments when I noticed I was sinking. The water was draining back into the lake – fast.

I swam into the middle of the room and by the time I got there my feet had touched the ground. It was seconds before the hole in the wall emerged and the remaining few feet of water drained out of it.

"Jesse!" I screamed into the empty room.

I heard a giggle and turned to find the child who had given me so much trouble standing on the stairs behind me, hands cupped over mouth. There were no secrets between us now.

In the light of the basement I could see her hair was wrapped behind her in a wet pony tail and her shorts and t-shirt had long ago rotted away or turned black with age, but I could tell they were mine all the same. The child I had thought a boy, had thought *Mike* of all people, was actually a girl. But she was ghost, I'd been right about that, the ghost of *me*; the part of me who had died in the lake all those years ago.

"Where's Jesse?" I asked it.

She giggled again and ran up the stairs. I chased her and by the time I reached the ground floor, she was gone. But I didn't need her to tell me where Jesse was - I knew where that hole led.

I ran outside onto the patio. I could see something moving impossible fast below the surface of the water toward the middle of the lake. I knew it was Jesse and the unholy creature who had taken him.

I made for the dock at a dead run and dove into the water at the end. The lake was even colder than the basement. I tried to ignore the chill as the ice crept into my fingers and toes, just like all those years before.

I swam for all I was worth but a part of me knew I couldn't save Jesse and that he was probably already dead. The numbness snaking up my arms and legs told me I wasn't going to make it anyway, but still I tried. I depleted every last ounce of energy I had to get to the middle of the lake. When I arrived there, I dove as deep as I could but the lake was pitch black underneath and no matter how far down I dove, I couldn't find the bottom. I found nothing. I felt nothing.

I looked back toward shore. There was nothing left to get me there but I started back toward my house anyway. The swim home took four times as long. I could see the little dead girl, standing at the edge of my dock, waving and smiling at me. I put my head in the water as I swam and tried to ignore the needle-thin stabs of ice.

When I finally reached the dock, the child was gone. The tide was in and I was able to pull myself up and drag my frozen limbs out of the water.

In was midday but the sun was somehow already setting and the temperature was dropping. I lay shivering on the dock, breathing hard but as quietly as I could manage. Not that it mattered. I knew she was watching me, somewhere, and probably laughing. This was her playground and the creature was her master. But he wasn't mine.

I forced myself up into a sitting position. If I had time, I would burn my fucking house to the ground but I was too tired and too cold and I had to get out of here. I couldn't bring myself to think about Jesse, or the horrible death that I had very likely caused. I pushed my fist against my chest as the pain took root there and began to grow. *No, not yet. Soon I will think about you, but not yet.*

Grabbing onto a tiki torch I pulled myself to a standing position and began to limp stiffly toward Sidetracks. Jesse's keys were my ticket out of here. I was halfway to the safety of the grass when the dock began to move underneath my feet. The water had risen several feet in as many minutes and there was something underneath the dock, pushing against it and tilting it to one side.

I never had a chance. I grabbed for one of the torches on the way over but it snapped in half as I was thrown back into the frigid water. The cold sliced through me like a knife.

I couldn't see it but I knew the creature was under the dock. I felt an unnatural undertow begin to pull me deeper down toward the underside of the structure and I kicked for all I was worth. I couldn't die this way, four feet from the beach and safety. I wouldn't.

If it had wanted me, it could have taken me then, but it was just a game. I escaped up to the surface and grabbed handfuls of the long grass on shore to pull myself up the frozen beach. I was up again and running within mere seconds of lifting my foot out of the water, fueled by adrenaline and little else.

I had to get those fucking keys. Jesse had used the last seconds of his life to throw them to me; I couldn't save him now but I could make sure he didn't die for no fucking reason.

I limped into Sidetracks hoping it was the last time I would ever darken its door. The keys were still lying against the wall where Jesse had thrown them. I stumbled into the hallway but when I reached down to pick them up, my stiff, frozen limbs overshot it and I accidently kicked the keys through the basement door and down the stairs where they slipped in between and fell to the cement floor below.

I sagged against the wall and sobbed. I could try to run, try to make it to town, but my body was exhausted. I wouldn't get more than a few hundred feet before I collapsed where I stood. And wherever I fell, that's where I'd be buried. I knew I probably wouldn't leave the basement alive, but I had to go down.

I could hear the flow of water in the room below as the lake slowly refilled the basement. I clutched the handrails for support and slowly descended, step by step, into the cavity below. The water was only knee deep but the room was still filling. The hole that I knew led to the lake was completely underwater again. If anything came through it I wouldn't know until it was too late.

I stumbled over to the corner underneath the staircase and shoved my hands into the water. They were still completely numb and I wondered if my fingers would even be able to feel the keys if I found them. My body was shuddering violently with chill and exhaustion. *Just a few minutes more. Just stay standing a few minutes more.* My teeth were chattering so loudly that the sound echoed around the room, drowning out the vicious lapping of the lake water against the walls.

But it didn't drown out everything. The sound of something surfacing from the water came from the corner directly behind me. I thrust my tongue in-between my teeth to try to quiet them. Tears made steaming hot trails down my cold face. It was over. *I* was over. I didn't want to die but if I had no choice then I didn't want it to hurt. *Please don't let it hurt.*

I knew it was the tall, deer-faced creature, and not the child. I felt a sickening, magnetic pull whenever the child was around, a symptom of our disgusting bond. But now - I only felt fear. I didn't want to see it, but I found myself turning toward the creature anyway. I lost my footing as I pivoted and when I stumbled forward my foot fell upon something sharp. The creature would know I had found them so I made no attempt to hide that I was picking them up. I braced a hand against a stair and bent down into the water. I couldn't feel my fingers at all so it was like playing the Claw Game at an arcade. It was long seconds before I finally pulled my hand up to see the silver key ring dangling on my finger. I quickly assessed my path to the stairway and thought I might make it before the creature could catch me. I thought I might try.

I couldn't help but look into the corner before running for the stairs. The thing was standing against the wall, as tall as the ceiling and dressed in some sort of heavy robe. Its antlers were long and sharp and its eyes were set so far back in the skull I couldn't make them out. And then suddenly it was gone. The creature had dropped down into the water as if it'd disappeared entirely from underneath its robes. A sob stuck in my throat and before I could take another step toward the stairs it grabbed onto my ankle. The creature's thin hand bit into my skin like barbed wire and I wasn't able to take a breath before I was pulled under the water with it.

My body was aching for air within seconds. I could feel it pull me out of the room through the hole in the wall and into a tunnel. The only thing I could think in such an impossible moment was: *Don't drop the keys. Don't drop the keys.*

We were moving fast but the tunnel was so long. It

wasn't even a minute before I felt my body succumb to the instinct to breathe. The water that I drew into my lungs was cold but all I felt was white-hot burning. The creature pulled me around sharp corners and through bottlenecks so impossibly tight I thought most of Jesse's bones must have broken when he was yanked through them.

I felt my body beginning to die. Even though I was in complete darkness the empty edges of my vision began to turn even blacker. The burning in my lungs ebbed away until I forgot where I was and what was happening to me. We've been told that Death's grip is cold and sharp, but that isn't true. It's warm and gentle, like a lullaby. I welcomed its soft touch. I surrendered to it.

But the demon's hold was even stronger. I was jerked upward so fast that I felt a bone snap in my leg. Cold air suddenly hit my face and my body pulled it into my lungs. As I coughed up murky, gray water, the darkness receded from the edges of my vision. I rolled over onto my back and laid there, floating in the water, only 30 yards from the shore.

The memory of my drowning had come back to me while I'd been under – the struggle, the pain, the desperation and fear as something pulled me down deeper and deeper. Evie was right: it was Mike who made it to the dock that day and it was me who never had.

But I couldn't remember the lost time, those hours that I'd spent at the bottom of the lake, dead as far as everyone knew. But I knew what had happened then. In the deepest part of the lake the creature had ripped my soul in two and kept one half for himself. He knew that I would one day come back, drawn by the bond like a moth to a flame.

I realized, too, then that the accusation and suspicion I

had seen on the faces of everyone at the beach that day had actually been fear. Fear of what I was.

As death slowly released its hold on me, pain began to bleed back in. And with it the instinct to live returned. *Fight. Run.*

I flipped over onto my stomach and started moving, slowly at first and then faster as I realized numbness could be an asset. I couldn't open my fists so I kicked with my uninjured leg and doggy paddled to the tall grass next to my dock. I dragged myself up the beach and then rolled over to catch my breath for the second time. My feet were still in the water, but I couldn't have made it another inch. My breathing didn't slow down but it gradually became more consistent. While I lay there I pried open my right hand and warm blood spilled down my wrist and forearm.

The serrated edges of the keys had burrowed into my skin and I had to manually pull my fingers back to get them out of my hand. Then I rolled over and pulled my legs out of the water. I was in more pain than I'd ever experienced in my life, but with maximum effort I was able to finally stand and hobble toward Jesse's truck.

I heard giggling bubble up behind me straight from the mouth of little, dead Casey. I catalogued her away along with all the other impossible things that had happened – a box to be opened and examined when I was far away from here.

I slammed into the side of the green truck and clutched the rearview mirror to keep from falling. *Almost there, almost there, almost there.* With my good hand, I flipped through the keys looking for the one with the Chevy symbol. I jammed it in the keyhole and turned until the lock popped open on the other side. His truck was so tall I had to conjure the strength from a place I didn't know I had to hoist myself up into the driver's seat. I screamed in pain as I dragged my broken, mostly severed foot into the cab and then righted myself in front of the steering wheel. I slammed the door shut and locked it.

Without bothering to look behind me I threw the truck in reverse. I tried to cut the wheel sharply to the right but my fingers wouldn't close over the steering wheel. I had to painstakingly make the turn with only the use of my wrists. As soon as I was clear of Jesse's house I pushed the shifter into drive and sped off over the grass toward the dirt road leading to town. There was nothing between me and the road and when I finally passed into the forest that surrounded the lake, I snapped. I laughed like an insane person; the sound so high-pitched and inhuman that I thought it couldn't be coming from me – but it was, and I couldn't stop it.

I was *free*. I wasn't going to die. I was going to be safe and warm soon. I slowed down to take the sharp left bend in the road without rolling the truck. On the other side of it was town – streets lamps burning, cars cruising, police with guns, hospitals, warmth and safety – except it wasn't. The truck had turned the corner but there was only blackness at the end of the road: darkness so deep and void that it looked like I was driving toward a black hole.

No. But it was too late. One second I was on the road and in the next I was in the air. The truck hit the water so hard I cracked my nose on the steering wheel. I heard it snap – more pain to flood my senses.

The truck was quickly sinking and I opened the door before the water pressure on the other side became too great. I fell out into the water - it wasn't so deep in this part of the lake. I could feel the lake floor underneath my feet and the faster I moved toward shore the more purchase I found. I was crawling toward the beach, only two feet of water between my body and the floor of the lake. But I long ago exhausted all the strength I had.

As I began to slow down, I considered just giving up. It was clear that I had never been meant to leave this lake, my fate had been sealed the day Aunt Evie drove me out of the woods. Why fight it? It was just going to hurt more in the end.

I was only a few feet away from a copse of reeds. But what would I do when I got there? Again pull myself up onto a cold beach? And for what? There was nowhere left to go.

Something snaked around my broken ankle sparking a new bout of crippling pain. I didn't bother to kick it off, I was done fighting. I was tired. I wanted sleep and warmth, and if that meant I'd have to do it in death, so be it. Jesse was dead because of me; drowned and broken. Why should my fate be any different?

I let go of the lake weeds I'd been holding and felt my body slowly turn over in the water. It wasn't the creature that had ahold of me this time, but the child. I hadn't seen her up close before. The girl's thin skin was stretched over her face like saran wrap on a sugar skull. Her hair was a mess of twigs and lake weed; tangled, dreaded, and turning white near her skull. But, she was me, there was no denying that. A corpse-like, rotting version of my past, but mine all the same.

The creature silently rose of out of the water several yards behind her; hardly causing a ripple in the surface of the lake. Its robe, I could see now, was black and crimson and seemed to shed water like the feather of a duck. His face was the bone-white skull of a buck and the horns that split off of his head were ebony. A thin, black hand appeared from the fold of the creature's robes. He held it out to me as his mouth fell open and a sound that may have been a scream rolled across the lake from shore to shore. My eyes flicked back to the little girl and she smiled at me. "Please," I whispered. Then I was dragged under and in the blackest part of the lake, I drowned.

*

Something warm was licking my face. The Anderson's dogs, Lake Calhoun. That's where I was. That's where I must be. I opened my eyes to the blinding light of day.

The water that lapped at my cheeks was warm; the sun overhead, scalding. I was floating on my back at the edge of the lake, body fractured and torn open. My skin was white and more heat was bleeding out of me every second. My hand grazed a reed on the shore.

I was alive. Why? Why was I still alive? I didn't want to be. I didn't want know how long I had been down this time. I didn't want to know what the monster had done to me. I could just sink. Sink to the bottom of the lake. No one would ever find me.

I turned over in the water and pulled myself out – one last time. I rolled onto my back and everything that had happened emerged unbidden from the void. The pain that broke over me like a wave was more excruciating than anything I was feeling in my body. All the death, all the horror, all the fear and pain. I wailed into the blue void above me. I screamed and sobbed until I convulsed. I cried until there was nothing left of me but my empty, broken body. And that was how Evie found me.

She dragged my body into the house. She set and

bound my leg. She set fire my cabin and to Jesse's, just like I had wanted. She carried me to the car and set me in the passenger seat. As we drove away from Sidetracks my eyes came to rest on the green pickup truck, almost fully submerged now, slowly sinking into the lake. The last of my humanity disappeared with it.

There is nothing left of me. Everything that remained of what I was had been expelled from my body the day I screamed in all into the sky. Evie is angry that I haven't said a word since she arrived at the lake that day. She doesn't understand that there is nothing left to speak for me.

She bought me a wheelchair, although I hardly ever leave her house. Only for doctor's appointments, she says. The thing that grows inside of me is part me, part Jesse, and part something else. Every month: a new doctor. Every appointment: the same. The ultrasound tech's smile fades into an uncomfortable frown and they fetch the doctor who speaks quietly with Evie. But I can hear them.

I'm so sorry. They say. *Please let us admit her, she's catatonic. It could be the shock.*

If I had the energy I would run away. If I had the heart I would abort the unholy creature inside me. But I have nothing except the hope that it will kill me when it's born. Aunt Evie has loftier dreams. She measures my stomach everyday as it grows and smiles happily when the thing moves or kicks her hand. She doesn't seem to care that the baby has no heartbeat.

ABOUT THE AUTHOR

C.K. Walker lives in Phoenix, Arizona with her family and four dogs. Read more of her stories at www.ck-walker.com.

Printed in Great Britain
by Amazon